CW01639538

Henrietta

THE SHACKLEFORD LEGACIES

BOOK FOUR

BEVERLEY WATTS

Copyright © 2025 BaR Publishing

© 2025 BaR Publishing. All rights reserved. No part of this publication may be reproduced, stored or transmitted in any form or by any means, electronic, mechanical, photocopying, recording, scanning or otherwise without written permission from the publisher.

It is illegal to copy this book, post it to a website, or distribute it by any other means without permission.
This novel is entirely a work of fiction. The names, characters and incidents portrayed in it are the work of the author's imagination. Any resemblance to actual persons, living or dead, events or localities is entirely coincidental.

BaR Publishing has no responsibility for the persistence or accuracy of URL's for external or third party Internet Websites referred to in this publication and does not guarantee that any content on such Websites is, or will remain, accurate or appropriate.

Designations used by companies to distinguish their products are often claimed as trademarks. All brand names and product names used in this book and on its cover are trade names, service marks, trademarks and registered trademarks of their respective owners. The publishers and the book are not associated with any product or vendor mentioned in this book. None of the companies referenced within the book have endorsed the book.

Cover art by wickedsmartdesigns

One

As one of King William IV's most trusted intelligence agents, Raphael Augustin couldn't deny that the discovery of a conspiracy to assassinate his Royal Majesty right under his very nose was at best embarrassing and worst...? Well, safe to say that twenty years earlier, it could very well have seen him clapped in irons and left to rot in his majesty's dungeons. That's if it hadn't cost him his head.

Fortunately, the King had cause to thank Raphael for previously preventing two assassination attempts against members of the Royal Family and exposing a plot to smuggle weapons to Irish rebels.

But while such an exemplary record might have saved his head, it certainly hadn't saved him from the blistering set down delivered by his majesty in the privacy of his bedchambers, after the garden party he'd been set to attend at the Duke of Blackmore's country seat was summarily aborted due to a failed assassination attempt by his grace's butler.

Neither had it helped that the man who'd ultimately saved the King's life was another Frenchman.

Indeed, Raphael's mood was further soured by the fact that as a result of said heroics, his countryman had spent the last four days on his deathbed, catapulting him from the hero of the day to hero of the decade.

And last but definitely not bloody least, Rafe had been left grinding his teeth after being instructed to offer Tristan Bernart a job once the investigation was finished...

Sighing, Raphael poured himself a large brandy from the decanter that had mysteriously appeared in his bedchamber two days earlier. There had been no note of explanation accompanying it, though Rafe suspected his royal set-down had been heard by everyone within a three-mile radius. Clearly, Nicholas Sinclair was not without sympathy. Which was just as it should be, since the whole bloody debacle had taken place under his roof.

Still, at least the King himself had finally departed with his entourage, leaving Raphael with the unenviable task of getting to the bottom of the whole deuced mess.

Lord Grey and the Duke of Wellington too had wasted no time before scurrying back to their own establishments, along with the rest of the guests – all evidently keen to ensure that they weren't unwittingly harbouring any unidentified *Revisionists* in their own households.

They would all be investigated by Raphael's network of agents over the coming months, as would the counterfeit Comte d'Ansouis who'd already been taken into custody. But first, Rafe needed as much information as he could get from the men who'd stumbled upon the conspiracy in the first place. While there was no evidence to suggest the *Revisionists'* plot had anything to do with the July uprising in France a year earlier, the overthrowing of the French King Charles X and the ending of the Bourbon restoration had undeniably resulted in a surge of revolutionary activity across Europe. The connection might seem unlikely, but nevertheless it couldn't be discounted without further investigation.

Unfortunately, getting an audience with the Duke of Blackmore was easier said than done. So far, Nicholas Sinclair had refused his request, citing the need for Tristan Bernart's presence during the interview process.

Which left Rafe twiddling his thumbs with only the Duke's in-laws for company. After three days, the Frenchman could only conclude that he'd never met a barmier family – and that was saying something, given that he'd lived in England since his parents had fled France during the Reign of Terror.

As a babe in arms, Raphael had had no idea that his family's exile had been carefully orchestrated by the British Intelligence services. Neither was he cognisant of the fact that his father had been what amounted to a spy for the British since well before Rafe's birth.

As minor French nobility, Etienne Augustin had enjoyed far more freedom for a much longer period than his wealthier counterparts, but perhaps inevitably, his name eventually came to the unfortunate attention of Jacobin fanatics, forcing him to escape with his family into the arms of France's greatest enemy.

Raphael had been raised and educated in England with the specific purpose of one day returning to gather intelligence on French émigrés, royalist plots and the ever-shifting political landscape of post-revolutionary France.

By 1831, Rafe occupied a unique position in London society. Publicly, he was a charming courtier and cultural advisor, while secretly, he monitored the French émigré community for signs of sedition, tracked the movement of revolutionary sympathisers and managed a network of informants across both England and France.

Which was why the recently unveiled *Revisionist* plot had come as such a shock. In truth, Raphael hadn't had even the faintest idea of their existence...

Henrietta loved all her cousins dearly, especially Roseanna and Francesca. The three of them had been close as children and were even more so now, though it had to be said that once they'd grown out of childish pursuits, Roseanna very often eschewed their threesome, preferring her own company. In truth, Henri had recently found herself a little worried that Rosie was turning into a recluse. Which just emphasised the old adage of never judging a book by its cover. How on earth her introverted cousin had managed to win the heart of a strikingly handsome Frenchman, who was apparently wealthy and certainly *no footman*, while simultaneously helping prevent a treasonous plot against the King, Henrietta had no idea.

And now, seated on a blanket next to Blackmore's lake watching them speaking together, Henrietta felt the first stirring of a completely unfamiliar emotion. Jealousy.

Frowning, she looked down at her lap, surprised to see her fingers twining themselves together. It felt as if they belonged to someone else.

How could she be jealous of her cousin's happiness? It went against everything that made Henrietta who she was.

Indeed, she'd always prided herself on being both practical and sensible, but with a well-developed sense of curiosity and a compassionate streak that admittedly sometimes got out of hand – the sheer number of waifs and strays employed at Redstone House gave testament to that.

Jealousy though? That had never been part of her character. But now, staring down at her twisting hands, she found herself wondering what would have happened if she'd met Tristan Bernart earlier. Before Roseanna.

Why hadn't her father introduced them? If he and Tristan had been friends and partners for as long as it was claimed, why had she never known about it? Biting her lip, Henrietta stilled her fingers and forced the uncomfortable feelings deep down inside. Her father had many business friends and acquaintances. It would have been strange indeed for him to introduce them all to his family.

Taking a deep breath, she looked up, making an effort to join in her cousins' banter. Peter was showing Victoria how to skim a pebble across the lake. Hampered by her skirts, Tory had requested Lilyanna's help in lifting the hem off the soft mud at the lake's edge and, to everyone's amusement, both women were in danger of tumbling directly into the cold water. Fortunately, Peter was able to drag them both away from the edge before disaster actually struck, but the accompanying hilarity had likely been heard back at the house.

As she watched, Henri found herself joining in the laughter, and to her relief, the unfamiliar jealousy faded. Shaking her head at her cousins' antics, she found her eyes travelling once more to the three figures standing in the distance. Clearly, Francesca was taking her role as chaperone very seriously, though she was facing away from the couple towards the lake.

Forcing her eyes away, Henrietta allowed her gaze to travel across the peaceful water. The day was warm but with the slightest hint of autumn, and the grounds were resplendent in their late summer adornment. Blackmore was beautiful at any time of the year and much grander than her family's home in Torquay. The difference had never seemed to matter though, and the entire extended Shackleford family had spent many wonderful summers swimming in the lake and playing in the fields and meadows.

Abruptly, Henri's gaze alighted on a small figure walking along the far edge of the lake. After a second, she realised it was the King's man. The one left behind to supposedly get to the bottom of the conspiracy. So far, her uncle Nicholas had kept him at arm's length due to Tristan Bernart's injury, but Henrietta guessed that now the counterfeit footman was up and about, King William's representative would want to hear about everything that had happened.

Watching the man's progress, Henrietta found herself wondering about him. She'd barely paid him any attention, preferring not to catch the eye of someone rumoured to be a spy for the King – though what she thought would happen if they actually exchanged a sentence, she wasn't entirely sure. It was merely that to her inexperienced eyes he looked dangerous. Though now she thought about it, she couldn't actually remember anything about his features. In her efforts to avoid attracting his attention, she'd barely allowed herself to look at him, let alone speak. She didn't even know his name.

As far as she was aware, he'd been taking his meals alone in his bedchamber – he'd certainly made little effort to socialise with the family. Likely he thought them all dicked in the nob. She found herself grinning again, wishing she could be present during the upcoming interview. Not that there was even the remotest chance of that – unless she could find somewhere within listening distance to eavesdrop.

The last week had been undeniably exciting, particularly to the younger members of the family, who'd been inclined to view the so-called conspiracy as a bit of a lark.

Until the bullet intended for the King had struck Tristan Bernart.

Henrietta shuddered as she remembered the sudden deafening silence after the shot rang out. Until that moment, no one had had the slightest indication that there was anything between Rosie and the supposed footman, and her abrupt, terrified cry had added another layer of unreality to what already felt like a fantasy.

During the days that followed, the sense that they were all living in a bizarre dream deepened, with the King demanding answers while his entourage searched every inch of Blackmore and Tristan fought for his life. It was only when the Frenchman was finally pronounced out of danger that the King returned to Whitehall, leaving his agent to pursue his enquiries. Though she hadn't seen it for herself, Henrietta had been told that the Comte d'Ansouis had been taken under armed guard back to London. She suppressed another shudder at the thought of what would likely happen to him as a traitor.

Henri shook her head to rid herself of such maudlin thoughts. The whole family were going their separate ways on the morrow, and she was determined not to spend the last day with her emotions tied up in knots. She looked over at Roseanna, who was now walking slowly along the path skirting the lake, back towards their picnic. She was arm in arm with her beau, who was plainly still recovering from his wound, while Francesca deliberately dawdled behind. Even from here, her happiness was palpable and in direct contrast to her earlier envy, Henrietta felt a sudden bubbling of joy for her reclusive cousin.

If such happiness could happen to Rosie, whose wont was not even to leave her bedchamber unless forced, then it could truly happen to any of them...

~

'Tare an' hounds, I think it's about deuced time Jenny and Brendan took you home,' Reverend Shackleford commented sourly.

'Ah dinnae ken wha' the devil ye mean.' Dougal Galbraith's tone was the epitome of innocence, even as the grin on his face told a completely different story. 'Ah bin thinkin' tae stay a wee bit longer, see a wee bit more o' Devonshire afore ah gae back tae Caerlaverock.'

The Reverend gazed at the Scot in horror. If Jenny and Brendan returned north without him, there was only one person who would be tasked with keeping the troublemaker in check. Augustus Shackleford gritted his teeth. Surely the Almighty wouldn't be expecting still more from him? Wasn't foiling yet another deuced treasonous plot enough to guarantee him celestial tea and toast when the time came? It had to be said that so far retirement was not turning out to be all the Reverend had hoped.

'Ah ken ye be a busy man, Augustus,' Dougal went on oblivious to his companion's expression, 'So dinnae fash yersel, ah'll nae bother ye.

'As ye ken, ah niver bin daft aboot all ye Sassenachs, an' ah bin thinkin' it be time ah put ma prejudices tae bed.' He waited for a second, likely expecting the Reverend to pat him on the back for such words of self-sacrifice. However, when the clergyman said nothing, Dougal frowned slightly before throwing his hands wide and declaring dramatically, 'As ye all be ma daughter-in-law's family, ah'm gaun tae stay wi all o' ye.

'An ah'll dae it one at a time...'

'I had not anticipated your family members departing quite so swiftly,' Raphael commented through gritted teeth. 'One evening to question everybody involved is not nearly enough time.'

Nicholas Sinclair stared at Augustin impassively. He gave no sign that it had indeed been a deliberate ploy on his part to keep the agent from questioning his family, though clearly the Frenchman suspected as much.

'We have told you everything we know,' he responded truthfully. 'I do not believe the conspiracy had anything to do with your countrymen aside from the fact that the *Revisionists'* leader was impersonating one.'

'You cannot say such a thing with certainty,' Rafe retorted, trying to keep his anger in check. He looked around the Duke's study. It was clear that none of the men in the room trusted him. 'And I cannot discount the fact that Monsieur Bernart here is also French.'

'As are you,' Jamie Fitzroy commented mildly.

'Why would he have gone to such lengths to save the King's life if he'd been part of the conspiracy?' In contrast, Adam Colborne's voice was clipped.

Rafe spread his hands, unable to contain his frustration. 'I am not your enemy, gentlemen. I am the King's man, tasked with ensuring his majesty's continued wellbeing.'

'And I applaud you for that,' Nicholas responded. 'However, you must understand our concern. We are not in the business of putting our families in harm's way. You have not been entirely truthful with us, Monsieur Augustin. You are not simply King William's man – you are the head of his intelligence agency, and I'm given to understand that your remit is to search out and deal with rumours of *French* insurrection. In my opinion, what happened here has nothing to do with events across the channel.'

Raphael felt a calmness settle over him. The Duke of Blackmore was no traitor - of that he was certain. But he could not be so sure of the others around the table. Especially the sea captain. Roan Carew had been tasked with rescuing the real Comte d'Ansouis together with the man who'd taken his place - Etienne Babin. Rafe very much doubted it was his only clandestine operation on French soil. And Tristan Bernart had been working for the man ever since.

But it was becoming very clear he would get nothing more in Blackmore. He would return to the King and ask permission to question Roan Carew further.

'What exactly dae ye think we could be guilty of?' Malcolm Mackenzie quizzed him. Rafe looked over at the grizzled Scot. For a reason he wasn't privy to - aside from the fact that the man had nursed Bernart back to health, the Duke's *valet* of all people had been invited to the table.

'It would be remiss of me to leave any stone unturned,' was all Raphael responded. 'I'm certain you are all very aware of *Les Trois Glorieuses* - the July revolution replacing King Charles X with his cousin Louis Philippe, the former Duke of Orléans. French insurrections rarely take place without some repercussions across the Channel.'

'Naturally we are cognisant of the *Three Glorious Days*,' Nicholas responded levelly, 'and you may rest assured that if any information comes to light connecting the *Revisionists* to the July Revolution in France, his majesty will be the first to know.'

Only partially satisfied, Raphael nodded and looked over at Tristan Bernart, who so far had said very little. The man's waxen appearance was clear evidence of the injury he'd sustained on behalf of his adopted sovereign.

'Do you remember anything of your childhood?' Rafe asked carefully. 'I'm referring to the time before you were imprisoned in Mont Saint-Michel?'

Tristan Bernart gazed steadily back, his expression inscrutable, and for a fleeting moment, another face flashed into Rafe's mind. An older, ruddier version of the man sitting in front of him. The agent frowned, and a second later the image was gone.

'I have vague memories of being in a house,' he responded with a shrug. 'More of a sense really than anything rooted in reality. I seem to remember ships too, though I'm uncertain whether my memories are showing me the Albatross.'

'That was Captain Carew's ship?' Raphael clarified.

Tristan nodded. 'My earliest memories – those I am certain of – are from my life aboard the Albatross.' He paused before adding, 'I cannot see how the time before my imprisonment is relevant to current events. I *am* sure I had never laid eyes on either D'Ansouis or Babin before I shared a cell with them.'

'How can you be so certain?'

The two men stared at each other, and the other, older face again showed itself briefly.

Somehow, somewhere, Raphael knew he'd seen that face before...

Two

In contrast to the delightful summer, early autumn in the coastal town of Torquay felt particularly dreary. September ended with a soggy wimp and a myriad of complaints that the newly laid pavements were for the most part impossible to walk on, overflowing with red mud and silt washed down from the red stone cliffs surrounding the town after the copious amounts of rain throughout the month.

Indeed, the thunderous downpours had been so insistent that it became almost impossible to walk anywhere at all, and even those with private transport quickly grew unwilling to risk staining their clothing with the awful red dye that would splash onto the bottom of breeches and hems of skirts, just by simply stepping down from a carriage.

Unsurprisingly, tempers in most households were at breaking point. Henrietta thought she would go mad if she had to spend one more day cooped up in the house. Emma and Joshua, her two younger siblings, were on the verge of killing each other – though it would be a close-run thing as to whether they or their father actually did the heinous deed. Fortunately for everyone concerned, Josh would shortly be returning to school for the Michaelmas term.

As a man accustomed to being out in all weathers, Roan Carew found the confinement particularly galling and spent much of his time closeted in his study.

The only highlight of the month was the invitation to Roseanna and Tristan's wedding, which had been scheduled to take place the following spring. Apparently neither the prospective bride or groom had been particularly happy about the delay, but Rosie's father - bringing the full weight of both his influence and his title as the Viscount Northwood – had insisted that his daughter's future marital home be entirely suitable before he walked her down the aisle.

In truth, it wasn't Gabriel Atwood's usual wont to exercise either his wealth or his standing, but given that his only experience of Tristan Bernart had been during the throes of a conspiracy, the Viscount was understandably concerned.

Naturally, Roan had vouched for the soon-to-be groom, having known him for more than twenty years, but Gabriel's response had been to mutter that that was the only reason the deuced Frenchman hadn't been thrown out on his ear...

Then, as September turned into October, and the ground became even more treacherous with piles of fallen leaves fusing with the endless mud, two things happened - both of which might well have served to alleviate the boredom but most definitely did nothing for the tension...

~

'You simply cannot leave him to make these visits alone.' Grace's voice had been unusually commanding, even shrill, and even now the Reverend couldn't believe he'd actually listened.

'It's not my fault Jennifer wed herself to a man whose father's dicked in the deuced nob. I can't possibly follow the rascal around the country. I have duties to take care of.'

'What duties?'

Reverend Shackleford groaned inside as he realised how neatly his daughter had trapped him. And to make matters worse, she'd threatened to withdraw his use of her husband's best carriage with the extra springs - the one he used to take him for his daily tankard of ale at the Red Lion - if he brought Dougal back before at least the end of October.

So now, here he was three weeks later on the fifth leg of a countrywide tour that had seen him practically thrown out of four of his offsprings' residences. Oh, they might not have couched it quite like that, but the excuses definitely rivalled many of the Canterbury tales he'd come up with over the years. Indeed, if he hadn't been so frustrated, the Reverend would have been seriously impressed. The only person who hadn't even bothered with a pretext was Patience, who'd told her father in no uncertain terms that if he didn't remove Dougal Galbraith from her home, she would ensure his removal in a box – family be damned. Augustus Shackleford knew his daughter well enough to realise she wasn't joking. Thunder an' turf, he'd raised a bunch of deuced harpies.

The Reverend looked over at his nemesis. The Scot was snoring in the opposite corner of the carriage, completely oblivious to the mayhem he'd caused – although the clergyman wasn't entirely sure whether Dougal was ignorant or didn't give a tinker's damn. But then, at least one of them was having fun.

With an inward sigh, Reverend Shackleford looked down at Flossy, currently snuggled up in his cassock. The little dog didn't care either, and her ever-increasing girth was ample evidence of how much she was enjoying herself.

Their carriage had left Ravenstone three days earlier and, by the Reverend's estimate, they would reach Torquay on the morrow. He'd been very evasive when speaking to Tempy about where they were headed, hinting that they'd likely return to Blackmore before deciding where to go next. Had he been foolish enough to name their destination, she'd have sent an urgent missive to Faith which would likely arrive at Redstone House before they did, thus providing Faith and Roan sufficient time to come up with an excuse to send them packing before they'd even arrived.

Grimacing, the Reverend found himself wishing he really could make a brief stop at Blackmore to see Percy. Even after all these years, his curate had the ability to make any problem seem slightly less insurmountable. It wasn't that Percy had ever provided much in the way of practical help whenever they found themselves in the suds - in truth he'd always been a bit of a chucklehead when it came to taking matters into his own hands - but somehow the Reverend had always come up his most impressive ideas when Percy was with him. As a result, they'd put a rub in the way of more than one blackguard involved in one kind of smoky business or another.

Augustus Shackleford leaned back against his son-in-law's luxurious upholstery, deep in thought. Would it be possible to make a quick stop in Blackmore without his wife Agnes finding out? A swift pint at the Lion with his oldest (and admittedly only) friend would go a long way to lightening his sour mood. But then, would Percy's wife Lizzy agree to keeping such a visit secret from Agnes? He'd be assured of a full month of curtain lectures if his beloved ever found out. It was a shame old Percy couldn't take a short holiday to join him in Torquay – it would certainly make the stay there more palatable.

Abruptly the Reverend sat forward, almost knocking Flossy off his lap. Why couldn't Percy join him for a week or two? Mayhap he could even bring young Finn with him?

Of course, under normal circumstances, the Reverend would sooner have donned a hair shirt for a month than give Dougal further opportunity to fill young Finn's ears with more totty-headed ideas, but he reasoned that even the Almighty would see this as an emergency.

But then, who'd take care of Percy's parish duties? That would be a tricky one. The last thing he wanted to do was to bring Blackmore to the attention of the Bishop of Exeter. The mutton-head still hadn't forgotten that havey-cavey business with Anthony's wife a few years earlier, and in truth, it was only the Duke's influence that had kept both him and Percy in a job.

The Reverend sighed. This would test even his legendary resources. He looked over at his still snoring companion, then outside at the rain lashed landscape. At the end of the day, it wasn't like he had anything else to do...

Raphael had purposefully offered no advance warning of his impending visit to the Carew household. If he wasn't expected, there was less chance of those being interviewed having the time to fabricate a bag of moonshine. In his experience, it was also the best way to encourage unguarded comments.

However, as his carriage finally came to a halt outside the Poulton's Hotel on Torquay's elegant Strand, he couldn't help wondering whether on this occasion, he'd made a grave error.

Rafe's upbringing had taught him to be suspicious of everything and everyone. His entire adult life had been spent watching for even the smallest signs of insurrection, inevitably leading to an innate distrust of even the most genuine of individuals.

He couldn't deny that his failure to unearth the Revisionist plot had been a blow to his pride, but perhaps at the end of the day that was no bad thing. It was possible that his successes over the past couple of years had made him overconfident. This was a timely reminder that he was neither invincible nor infallible.

There was in truth no evidence that Roan Carew was a traitor. His record as Captain of HMS Albatross during the Napoleonic wars had been exemplary and since then he'd been a businessman of exceptional moral character as well as being a close friend and relative of not one, but five peers of the realm – all of whom had risked their lives at one time or another for their King and Country.

So why the bloody hell was he here?

Raphael gritted his teeth as the carriage door was opened. Climbing down, he nodded to the two ostlers as they heaved his trunk off the roof, one carrying it into the hotel while the other climbed up next to his coach driver to direct the carriage and horses to the stable yard.

Carefully picking his way over the muddy cobbles, Rafe eventually found himself in an unexpectedly comfortable lobby. The wet day outside meant that the meagre late afternoon light barely penetrated beyond the front door, but the candleholders with their flickering lights gave a most welcome ambience to a delightfully appointed wood-panelled reception hall.

Ten minutes later he was shown into a small but tastefully decorated bedchamber. His trunk had already been placed in the room, and a cheerful fire burned in the large fireplace.

Sighing, he pulled off his boots and threw himself down on the bed.

Why was he here?

The last thing he needed right now was to antagonise the powerful Duke of Blackmore by hounding the peer's relatives - and turning up unannounced at the sea captain's home simply to catch Carew out, would surely reach his grace's ears. Simple etiquette demanded that, at the very least, he send a note announcing his presence in Torquay. Though of course, a polite note would not guarantee him an audience.

But at the end of the day, what exactly was he hoping to learn? Had he become fixated on looking for connections when there were none? A hostage to his damned pride?

Rafe wasn't accustomed to questioning himself or his motives. He'd always viewed his decisiveness as one of his greatest strengths. But if that same decisiveness had turned to arrogance, he wouldn't last much longer in the dangerous game he played.

Raphael allowed his mind to drift. He found that doing so often led him down paths to solutions he would otherwise have missed.

At length, a face popped into his head. Frowning, he focused his mind on the image, seconds later recognising it as Tristan Bernart. Tristan Bernart - but not quite. It was the face he'd seen when he'd looked at his countryman back in Blackmore, and all of a sudden, he knew who it was. Rafe sat up.

His instincts emphatically told him that Roan Carew was no traitor. But, putting his vanity aside, he hadn't been able to rid himself of the gut feeling that there was *something* here. Perhaps it had nothing to do with the *Revisionists*, but it was definitely connected to the man who'd helped unmask them.

Tristan Bernart. An unknown orphan, who Rafe would wager his entire fortune, was somehow a relative of the once powerful, now deceased, Marquis de Montclair.

~

Augustus Shackleford couldn't deny that the solution he finally came up with bore no comparison to the Banbury stories he'd concocted during his heyday, but in fairness, these days he often had trouble remembering his own name.

On stopping to partake of a light lunch in Ashburton, he asked for a quill and paper, and after careful thought, wrote a short missive requesting Percy's immediate presence in Torquay to assist him in dealing with an urgent spiritual matter involving their dear friend, Dougal Galbraith. Pausing after the words *spiritual matter*, Reverend Shackleford wondered whether adding the possibility of possession might be doing the whole thing a bit too brown. Of course, where Dougal was concerned, it wasn't entirely beyond the realm of possibility, but there was a risk that the Almighty might consider it a step too far.

At the moment, the letter was not a complete bag of moonshine – there had been more than one occasion the Reverend had had spiritual concerns involving the old Scot, although mostly it centred around his own immortal soul when he'd been tempted to wring Dougal's neck.

Finally, deciding he might as well be in for a penny as a pound, he finished by stating that if Percy felt that Finn's Christian Education might well benefit from a spot of exposure to the forces of evil, then he should undoubtedly bring the boy along. (In fairness, he didn't actually write the word *possession*...)

Staring down at his handiwork, the Reverend tapped the feathered quill against his chin thoughtfully. Percy would undoubtedly know that something smoky was afoot – mainly due to the fact that the letter referred to Dougal as their *dear friend*, but if he hadn't included such a complete plumper, the curate might have been inclined to ignore the missive entirely.

He could only hope the Almighty would simply consider the sentiment encouraging, and overlook the bit about the forces of evil...

Three

Henrietta was the first to spot the Duke of Blackmore's carriage as she was heading upstairs to fetch her book after dinner and for a few seconds she thought it was her aunt and uncle. However, as the door opened and Flossy jumped out, she realised at least one of the passengers had to be her grandfather.

Sure enough, seconds later the little dog was followed down the steps by Augustus Shackleford, and close behind... Dougal Galbraith? What on earth was her cousin Jennifer's father-in-law doing here?

Henri stared in disbelief, wondering if the rain had finally sent her addled. She thought back to how the Scot had set up almost everyone's bristles at Blackmore. His unexpected arrival here along with the Reverend of all people was likely to put her father in a worse dudgeon than he already was. Feeling an impending sense of doom, she hurried to find her mother...

'Well, given the dreadful weather over the last few weeks, I can imagine you must be thanking the Almighty for sending me and Dougal to alleviate the deuced monotony,' the Reverend commented jovially as they waited for refreshments in the drawing room. The resulting stony expression on his son-in-law's face was anything but thankful. In fact, Roan looked as though he'd been sucking a lemon. Augustus Shackleford sighed inwardly. It was hardly surprising really, turning up unannounced as they had. But then, the expressions of those who'd actually been expecting them had been little better. Seriously, it was enough to give a man an attack of the mulligrubs.

'Of course, it's lovely to see both you and Dougal, Father, though it would have been nice if you'd sent us notice of your impending visit,' Faith answered, clearly resigned to making the best of a bad job. The Reverend didn't miss the hard look she cast towards her Friday-faced husband, and after a second, the sea captain offered a smile of welcome, albeit through gritted teeth. Given that Roan was evidently trying to make an effort, the clergyman wasn't sure now would be a good time to mention that Percy and Finn might well be joining them...

Instead, he gave a small cough and murmured, 'Didn't you receive my letter?' He could see Dougal's raised eyebrows from the corner of his eye, but before the Scot had the chance to land him in the basket, a knock on the door heralded the fortunate arrival of tea and a small cold collation for their impromptu guests.

'Didn't Grandmama object to you visiting us without her?' Henrietta asked curiously once the tea had been poured and handed round.

Before her grandfather had a chance to reply, Dougal gave a loud guffaw as he helped himself to a large piece of shortbread. 'Ah ken ye all be acquentit wi' the bonny Agnes,' he chuckled, waving the biscuit towards his scowling companion, 'An' ah'd wager ma life savins the bampot didnae tell her.' Still grinning, he shook his head and dipped the shortbread into his tea before pulling out the soggy lump remaining and sucking on it enthusiastically.

There was a pause as everyone looked expectantly at the clergyman, whose face was turning an interesting shade of puce.

'You may not be aware, but Agnes works very closely with Mr Grimshaw, the local apothecary,' Reverend Shackleford growled at length, throwing a murderous look towards his grinning travelling companion. 'And unfortunately found it impossible to excuse herself from her obligations at this time.'

Faith shook her head and gave a loud sigh. 'Really, Father, I think perhaps you would do well to discourage such an alliance – it's only down to sheer luck that Stepmother hasn't succeeded in poisoning the entire village.'

She looked expectantly at her father, who had the grace to look sheepish. After a second, he threw his hands in the air, before giving a resigned sigh and helping himself to another biscuit. 'There's no chance of that,' he muttered. 'Old Grimshaw gives her bottles filled with coloured water to test.'

'Why on earth does he do that?' Faith asked in bewilderment.

'Because I pay him,' was the Reverend's blunt response. 'A pretty deuced penny it costs me too. But it's either that, or...' He paused before adding in a strangled tone, '*Conversation.*'

There was another, lengthier silence, eventually broken by Dougal slapping his thighs in delight. 'Augustus Shackleford, ah truly didnae think ye had it in ye,' he chuckled. 'Ah be thinkin' this calls fer a wee dram.' He looked at Roan before directing his gaze pointedly towards the brandy decanter on the sideboard.

Roan looked flatly back, fighting a sudden illogical urge to grin. Perhaps the Almighty had indeed sent the two reprobates to break the monotony – a rousing argument was certainly better than staring at the never-ending rain. He was just about to climb to his feet when the doorbell rang. Frowning, he sank back into his chair and waited. A caller at this time of night was unlikely to be bringing good news.

A minute or so later, a knock on the door heralded the arrival of their housekeeper. 'A note for you, sir,' Mrs Bellamy informed him, hurrying over with a large envelope. 'It's from the Poulton's Hotel. The lad is waiting on the step for an answer.'

Roan glanced over at his wife, guessing her apprehensive expression was a match for his. Seconds later, any burgeoning joviality vanished. He looked over at Faith. 'Raphael Augustin is in Torquay and requesting an audience.'

For the first time in weeks, the following morning dawned sunny and crisp and, determined to take advantage of the sunshine while it lasted, Henrietta offered to take Flossy for a walk immediately after breakfast. Fortunately, her mother had already arranged to take Emma to the modiste, which meant that Henri had some time to herself away from the house for the first time in what felt like forever.

As she walked down the drive, Flossy happily rooting in the undergrowth beside her, Henrietta reflected on the unexpected events of the previous day. The knowledge that the King's agent was in Torquay asking questions had sent a thrill of fear right through her, though in truth, she didn't know why – it wasn't as if her father had done anything wrong. She remembered her feelings about the Frenchman back at Blackmore – her instinct that Raphael Augustin was not a man to be crossed.

That her father was of the same opinion, she had no doubt, though he'd said very little on receipt of the note. After responding with an invitation for afternoon tea on the morrow – which was now today – he'd retreated to his study while the rest of them had retired to their respective bedchambers.

Pursing her lips, Henrietta opened the gate and stepped out onto the street, determined to put all thoughts of King's men and spies out of her mind. It was wonderful to be outdoors, despite the morass underfoot. However, as she turned the corner onto the main thoroughfare leading down to the harbourside, the mud unfortunately became much thicker, having accumulated into a thick layer of sludge liberally mixed with rotting leaves and horse dung.

After a few yards, she was forced to pick Flossy up lest the little dog disappear completely into the foul-smelling muck. As she picked her way, she struggled to tuck Flossy underneath her arm whilst using her hands to hold up the hem of her skirt. Henrietta only hoped the waterfront promenade had at least been cleared of detritus. Any euphoria she'd felt at being out of the house slowly vanished – along with the sunshine.

Muttering to herself, Henri kept her eyes firmly on the ground. If she slipped over here, *she* might never be seen again – never mind Flossy. After what felt like hours, the road finally began to level out enough for her to risk taking her eyes off the treacherous ground. To her relief, the beginning of the promenade was only about fifty yards away.

And then it started to rain.

Henrietta gave a low moan. The one thing she hadn't brought with her was an umbrella, and even if she had, she'd have been hard pushed to hold dress, dog and canopy. Her bonnet, sadly, was not made for sudden downpours. She didn't know whether to stamp her feet or simply cry, but a temper tantrum wouldn't stop her from getting soaked. After a second, she pursed her lips, put her head down and took a step forward... only for her foot to slide out from underneath her due to the sudden deluge. She emitted a most unladylike shriek as she fell backwards directly onto her posterior, where she sat in an ignominious heap, still gripping a now wriggling Flossy.

Seconds later, a carriage and four sailed straight past her prone form, liberally splashing her from head to toe with mud and goodness knew what else.

Her humiliation was complete, and since stamping her foot was no longer an option, she decided that tears would do perfectly well.

A moment later, just as her self-pitying wail was about to reach epic proportions, a shadow fell across her. Gulping she looked up... into the ice-blue eyes of Raphael Augustin.

'Do you intend to sit there for the rest of the day, Mademoiselle, or may I assist you to your feet?'

Flossy wriggled even harder as Henrietta found herself saying the most ridiculous words ever uttered. 'I'm perfectly fine, thank you, Sir,' before wanting to bite out her tongue.

He raised his eyebrows – undoubtedly at her ridiculousness, before murmuring, 'I think perhaps both your dog and your... *derrière* might disagree with you, Miss Carew.'

He knew who she was. She'd been wrong earlier; her humiliation was *now* complete.

'Please allow me to assist you, Mademoiselle.' His voice was studiously polite, giving no hint that he considered her a complete mutton-head, and after the briefest of seconds, Henri gave a small sniff and gripped his proffered hand, allowing him to pull her to her feet. Nonsensically, the only thing running through her mind as he tugged was how lean, tanned and *warm* his fingers were.

Without hesitation, he lifted the now shivering Flossy out of her arms and tucked the little dog under his. 'My hotel is across the road, Miss Carew. Allow me to accompany you into the warmth where I am certain they will have the means to... err, dry you out somewhat.'

Having lost the will to live somewhere between her absurd declaration of well-being and his mention of her backside, Henrietta allowed herself to be propelled across the road into the blessed warmth of the Poulton's Hotel Lobby where she was fortunately very quickly ushered into a private room by two female members of staff. Minutes later, all but her undergarments had been removed, whisked away to be cleaned and replaced with a skirt and blouse embroidered with the words *Poulton's Hotel*.

Though tempted to remain hidden away from prying eyes –two piercingly blue ones in particular - Henrietta abruptly remembered her rescuer still had hold of Flossy. She uttered a small gasp. How could she have forgotten? Who knew what kind of treatment the little dog would receive from someone who *spied* on people for a living? She ignored the little voice in her head declaring that Flossy had been paw deep in one havey cavey business after another since the day she came to Blackmore - at least her grandfather was a man of the cloth. Hurrying after the two ladies, she pulled open the door to the lobby, ready to snatch the little dog from the jaws of death – or at the very least being taught even more unsavoury habits - only to pause on the threshold in surprise.

Her grandfather had always boasted about Flossy's excellent judge of character, stating it had come from being originally owned by a *blasted traitor* who'd apparently been involved in a plot to assassinate the King George IV. The clergyman's declaration had come after imbibing a little too much brandy one Christmas Eve, and it had been the source of endless speculation and not a little frustration between the cousins since once he'd sobered up the following day, he'd refused to breathe another word on the subject – as had everyone else involved.

But still, from the little she knew, the fact that the little dog was now curled up on Monsieur Augustin's lap snoring happily was a good indication that the King's man was *truly* the King's man and not a blackguard intent on purposely ruining her father's good name.

Concealed as she was by the door, Henrietta found herself deliberately studying the Frenchman's features for the very first time. After a few seconds, she drew in a shallow breath. How had she never noticed how handsome he was? His face was tanned, causing her to wonder if he'd spent much time in warmer climes. High cheekbones and a chiselled jaw gave a clear indication of his aristocratic heritage, and even from here, she could tell that his eyes were the blue of a summer sky. A head of dark chestnut hair tied carelessly back in a queue in defiance of current fashion completed the picture. Though well dressed, he was evidently no slave to style.

Abruptly his eyes swivelled towards her hiding place, and though she was almost certain he couldn't see her, she found herself colouring up. What the devil was wrong with her? Handsome he might be, but she was under no illusions concerning his potential ruthlessness should he deem it necessary.

As his eyes drifted elsewhere, she took another, much deeper breath and stepped past the open door into the hotel lobby. As she approached, his head quickly swivelled back towards her, but Flossy, the little wretch, didn't even bat an eyelid. If anything, her snoring got louder.

'Thank you for your assistance,' she stammered, adding an uncertain, 'Monsieur,' to her sentence. To her surprise his mouth quirked.

'We are in England, *Miss* Shackleford so feel free to speak the language of your countrymen - though as you undoubtedly noticed earlier, I often forget where I am.' He bent his head in acknowledgement of her effort, but the amusement in his eyes remained and her previous colour was nothing to the fiery red of her face now.

He waved towards the vacant chair on the opposite side of the small table in front of him. 'Please take a seat. I have taken the liberty of ordering some tea.'

After a slight hesitation, Henrietta sat down, smoothing her borrowed clothes self-consciously.

'It's not often that Flossy lets her guard down so quickly,' she murmured after a moment, waving towards the comatose animal.

He looked down and stroked the silky head. 'I have always wanted a dog,' he mused, 'but alas my lifestyle has never allowed me the indulgence of a canine companion.'

'I would have thought that a dog would have been of help in the work that you do,' Henrietta responded carefully. 'I have read that they can help with all manner of things, from sniffing out dangerous substances to defending one against charlatans and ruffians.' She sat forward. 'Take Flossy for example. She has been of tremendous assistance to my grandfather. Indeed, she helped bring Etienne Babin to justice when he would have fled.'

'Oh? And how did she do that?' Raphael queried, his voice deceptively mild. Observing his raised eyebrows, Henrietta abruptly realised she may have unintentionally given away too much. Worse, his interested expression told her it was too late to take the words back. With an internal grimace, she gave a small, self-conscious cough and explained.

'I believe she – Flossy, that is - she... err... well, she took a rather large chunk out of the varmint's ankle,' The last was said in a rush before Henri winced, adding hastily, 'That's not to say Flossy is vicious you understand. Why, she's simply the sweetest little dog to people she knows...' *Fiend seize it, that didn't sound right.* Henrietta began to colour up again as she struggled to come up with words that didn't make Flossy sound like a diminutive hellhound - finally, finishing weakly, 'Grandfather has always said she's an excellent judge of character. As I mentioned, she certainly appears very taken with you.'

As if on cue, Flossy looked up and gave a soft growl. Fortunately, she followed it with an enthusiastic wag of her tail as she caught sight of the plate of biscuits coming towards them. Henrietta looked gratefully up at the bellboy as he carefully placed the tea tray onto the table. 'Do you wish me to pour, Miss?' he asked with a small bow.

Henri nodded, grateful she didn't have to risk adding her inferior tea-pouring skills to her growing list of faux pas – though why on earth it should matter, she had no idea.

All too quickly, the bellboy retreated, leaving the two of them alone again. Now that the subject of dogs had been exhausted, Henrietta had no idea what to say. Under normal circumstances, she was reasonably well versed in the art of conversation, but really, what did one chat about to a King's Spy? Earlier, she'd been well on the way to declaring Flossy a vicious killer... The little dog gave a loud snore, plainly unconcerned about her close brush with death.

'I'm given to understand there is to be a family wedding in the Spring?' Her companion broke the silence after a few uncomfortable moments.

'Indeed,' Henri responded with a smile. 'We are all very much looking forward to it.'

'Including her father?' Raphael asked, the doubt very evident in his voice. Henrietta twisted her hands in her lap, realising she needed to choose her next words carefully. If she proclaimed her uncle delighted, he would no doubt believe she was lying.

She gave a small shrug. 'I think my cousin would have preferred the wedding take place before Christmas, however my uncle, understandably wishes to ensure that Mr Bernart is in a position to take care of his daughter and has merely asked that he purchase an appropriate property before the nuptials take place.' Her answer was honest, as far as it went. In truth, it had been a little more convoluted than that.

Raphael Augustin's lips twitched again, but this time Henrietta felt an unaccountable urge to slap the smirk off his face. Clearly, he was well aware she was dissembling.

'Your father is well acquainted with Bernart, non?' This time his use of French told Henrietta the question was important – he might be a bloody spy, but he wasn't the only one who could recognise a *tell*.

'Indeed, they have known one another for many years,' Henrietta responded with a false smile, 'as I'm sure my father mentioned to you the last time you spoke to him. He rescued Mr Bernart as a mere boy and took him on – initially as a cabin boy, I believe.' She paused to take a sip of her tea, then, looking over the rim of her cup, she added, 'As far as I'm aware, their friendship is one of mutual trust and has developed over many years.'

Finally, putting her cup decisively back onto its saucer, she straightened her shoulders and continued. 'I thank you for your timely intervention, Mr Augustin, and of course for the tea, however, if it has stopped raining, I will take my leave. My parents will be getting concerned at my continued absence.'

'You will walk home in your borrowed uniform?'

'I am certain the hotel will not object to having my own garments sent to the house once I provide my name and address,' Henrietta retorted, 'and naturally I would not return the ones I am wearing without them being washed and pressed.'

'It does not bother you to be seen as working class?' He had not moved, and neither had the dratted dog. Really, the man was insufferable, not to mention boorish.

'Why on earth should it?' she snapped. 'I think you misunderstand my situation, *Monsieur*, I might have relatives who are fortunate enough to have a title, but my father is a former naval officer turned trader and my mother the daughter of a country vicar. I have no cause for absurd airs and graces.'

He stared at her impassively for a second before bending his head slightly in acknowledgement of her words 'Will you be warm enough without your coat?' was all he said.

She got to her feet. 'My shawl did not get wet, and it is not particularly cold. I am certain it will suffice. Thank you again for your assistance, Sir. *Come Flossy*.'

At the sound of her name, the little dog finally looked up. Then, giving a small yawn, jumped nonchalantly to the floor. Henrietta stepped around the table, intending to pick up the now-trailing lead.

Unfortunately, instead of gathering it up, she inadvertently trod on it, just as Flossy caught sight of a cat slinking through the front door. With a furious bark, the pooch took off towards her quarry, causing Henri to overbalance and fall backwards, *again*, but this time directly into Raphael Augustin's lap...

Four

'I do not think you are the kind of man who would wish to waste the next hour in polite conversation, Mr Augustin, so, I will go ahead and ask the question. Why are you here?'

Roan's query was delivered with freezing politeness, almost incongruous as they regarded each other over their bone China teacups.

However, if he was hoping to catch the Frenchman off guard, he was disappointed. Raphael was more than accustomed to those he questioned attempting to put him at a disadvantage. And on this occasion, he'd already decided to lay all his cards on the table.

Which, of course, had nothing at all to do with the events of the morning...

Since being shown into the drawing room, Rafe had deliberately avoided looking over at Henrietta Shackleford. He had no idea whether she'd revealed anything at all about their impromptu meeting but thought it extremely unlikely that she'd spoken of her ignominious fall into his lap. Indeed, the chances of anyone actually having witnessed the event were slim to none, since she shot off his knees like all hell was after her. But then, the problem was not what actually happened, but his reaction to it...

Rafe gritted his teeth, then forced himself to relax. The occasional schoolboy reaction to the feel of an attractive woman against him was not something to be concerned about.

Deliberately taking his time, he finished his tea and placed the empty cup back on the table. Then, leaning against the back of his chair, he regarded the occupants of the room with a calmness he was far from feeling inside.

He couldn't deny it was a good turnout. Not only was Roan Carew and his eldest daughter present but also his wife and, if Rafe's memory served him correctly, the father-in-law clergyman. The only person whose identity he couldn't quite place was a wild-looking Scotsman who seemed to think the whole proceedings were an entertaining diversion put on specially for him, if his delighted grin was anything to go by.

Raphael knew his next words would be the very last ones his audience would be expecting. He leaned forward, saying simply, 'Captain Carew, I have reason to believe that the man you know as Tristan Bernart is, in fact, Tristan Antoine de Montclair, the son of Philippe and Catherine de Montclair, and the lost heir of the Montclair family.'

Raphael had been prepared for the tumult his words would create and watched Roan Carew's face carefully as he spoke, but other than a slight widening of his eyes, the sea captain did not seem particularly shocked by the revelation. Had he already known?

After a few seconds, as the clamour at his revelation died down, Roan spoke. 'I cannot say I'm entirely surprised.' His voice was thoughtful more than anything. Rafe raised his eyebrows but did not interrupt. 'From the very moment he joined my ship, there was a... presence about him. He rose through the ranks quickly – only his age held him back from making it to full captain by the time he was twenty.'

'I didn't realise he commanded a ship,' Rafe retorted.

Roan shook his head. 'He didn't. After I retired from the Royal Navy, I asked Tris to join me as my business partner. I've never for one moment regretted it.' There was a pause before Roan added, 'It was during one of our business dealings that he crossed paths with Babin again. By then, the charlatan was passing himself off as the Comte d'Ansouis.'

'But Bernart realised he was not the real Comte.' Raphael confirmed.

Roan nodded. 'He recognised the varmint immediately. The rest I believe you already know.' There was a pause before he asked the question Rafe had been waiting for.

'Why do you believe Tristan is the missing Marquis de Montclair?'

Raphael was silent for a moment. 'Philippe de Montclair was a friend of my father,' he answered finally. 'I met him on numerous occasions before my family fled to England. As soon as I laid eyes on your man Tristan Bernart, I was struck by a sense of familiarity, though at first, I couldn't recall where I'd seen his face before. Yesterday it finally came to me.'

'You say this even though the last time you met the Marquis de Montclair was as a child? I think you are gambling with your reputation, Mr Augustin.' Roan's voice wasn't quite scathing, but it was close.

'Believe me, I do not speak of this lightly,' Rafe retorted, his voice tight. 'If you will permit me to continue, I'll explain why I have come to you without first verifying my beliefs.' He paused, staring directly at Roan. 'I know you do not trust me, Captain Carew, but believe me, in this I have your friend's continued well-being at heart.

'That both Philippe and Catherine de Montclair were murdered in January 1806 in cold blood is certain, but the body of their only son was never discovered. Nor was any trace found of the men who committed the murder. As far as I can tell, the chateau lay empty for the next couple of years, until a supposed distant cousin suddenly appeared and has occupied the chateau ever since. While he's never proclaimed himself the heir, he has enthusiastically assumed the role of supposed *caretaker* of the Montclair estates.

'But consider this – Philippe de Montclair wielded significant power in both *Bretagne* and *Normandie* at the time of his death, and the Montclair coffers were reputedly filled to bursting. The Chateau and Estate are situated close to the town of Lannion in Bretagne - approximately one hundred and twenty kilometres from Mont Saint-Michel as the crow flies and a three-day carriage ride. However, the Marquis also had a second, much smaller chateau just outside the small town of Pontorson, which is much, much closer - a mere nine kilometres from Mont Saint-Michel. It is perfectly possible to believe that at the time of the attack, someone loyal to the family took Philippe and Catherine's child from Montclair, with the intention of taking him to the chateau in Pontorson.

'Unfortunately, that property too was left a smoking ruin just over a year later – it's feasible to think the attackers might have been looking for the child, but if they were, they had no luck. Philippe de Montclair's son remained missing – until now.

'Let us speculate that the boy survived and was forced onto the streets – where he somehow survived for nearly two years. Tristan himself remembers being caught and imprisoned for stealing an apple – but he doesn't know how long he'd been locked up for before Babin and the Comte d'Ansouis' arrival. It couldn't have been that long. A boy with his background wouldn't have lasted in that hellhole more than a few months at most.

'Which takes us to July 1808, when the Albatross was at anchor waiting to bring a freed French prisoner to England...' He trailed off, allowing his audience to draw their own conclusions.

'Do you believe it possible that Etienne Babin was part of the group who murdered Philippe and Catherine Montclair?' Faith asked, speaking for the first time.

Before Rafe had a chance to answer, Roan interrupted. 'You actually believe that the lost Montclair family heir somehow ended up in a cell with a member of the group who murdered his family?' The sea captain's voice was incredulous. 'Could it be you are actually seeing connections where there are none?'

'Of course. I do not have a crystal ball, but I think my theory is far more probable than believing the *Revisionists* simply sprang up out of thin air in England,' Raphael answered curtly. 'I know that the Duke of Blackmore - perhaps understandably - believes that the conspiracy did not originate across the channel, but...'

'...He is not aware of the attack on the Montclair estates,' Faith finished. Raphael inclined his head.

'So, who do you think gave the order to free d'Ansouis – the real one that is?' The Reverend's blunt question cut to the heart of the matter.

'My orders came from impeccable sources,' Roan commented tightly.

'I don't doubt it,' Rafe replied coolly. 'And we may never know whether d'Ansouis was merely in the wrong place at the wrong time and fell victim to a conspiracy he had no idea existed. Was whoever organised the extraction from the *Bastille of the Seas* wishing to save the Comte or use him?' He looked over at Roan. 'My guess is that you were never told exactly who ordered the rescue, or how it was that Babin was present to accompany him – a criminal who would be very unlikely to have any sympathy towards an aristo locked up by the regime.'

There was a short silence as the rest of the room took in the Frenchman's sober words.

'I think it is pastime to stop equivocating and tell us exactly what you are thinking,' Roan grated, his anger finally getting the best of him. 'For pity's sake, say what's in your damned head, man.'

Raphael sighed. The Englishman was right, it really was time to speak frankly. He stared downwards, gathering his thoughts for a few seconds, before choosing his words carefully. 'The Marquis de Montclair was a wealthy man – money that had been amassed over many generations,' he told them after a moment. 'And like many of the old families fearing the revolution, he converted almost his entire fortune into gold and precious stones. It was easy to hide – much safer than leaving the money in a bank that could be confiscated at a moment's notice.'

'So how the deuce did you know about it?' Reverend Shackleford questioned. 'I doubt the fellow would have announced it to every Tom, Dick and Harry.'

'Philippe confided to my father.' Rafe's retort was short and to the point. 'May I continue?'

'Please, Father, let Mr Augustin finish,' Faith added, glaring at her parent as he opened his mouth to say something else.

Nodding his head in thanks for her intervention, Raphael continued. 'The Marquis also had a very long reach when he chose to exercise it.

'Let us consider the possibility that the attackers were looking for capital to further their ambitions - feasibly spanning both sides of the Channel - whilst ridding themselves of a potentially powerful adversary.'

'How can you be sure that these men gained access to Montclair's wealth?'

'I was aware that the alleged cousin first appeared at Montclair in August 1808, almost immediately after d'Ansouis and Babin were freed. The man has always maintained that the bulk of the Montclair fortune was lost, and I have no evidence to say otherwise - aside from the fact that the man appears to have lived quite comfortably since his sudden rise in fortune. There had been no reason to investigate the matter further – until now.'

'But that doesn't mean he's involved in a damned conspiracy,' Roan protested.

'No, it doesn't. But if he is truly a blood relative of Philippe Montclair, why has he never proclaimed himself the new Marquis? Certainly, no one else has come forward to lay a claim.

'My suspicion is that he purposely continues with the role of caretaker. While he has no title, nothing is expected of him, and he's able to remain in relative seclusion. No one is asking any questions, and no one is paying any attention to his comings and goings. In short, the man might as well be invisible.'

Rafe paused and looked round at his audience. He could finally see understanding in the eyes of all.

There was every chance that the Revisionists were not finished but had gone underground to regroup. Babin had not been their leader – merely a lieutenant.

And finally, somebody high in the British government, possibly close to the King, could well be a traitor...

It was Henrietta who spoke first. 'Could Tristan be in danger?'

'Naturally the last thing the conspirators would want is for the heir to the Montclair title to suddenly appear, alive and well. Once they get wind of it, I think it a very distinct possibility they will immediately take whatever steps they deem necessary,' Raphael answered truthfully.

Roan stood up abruptly and went over to the sideboard. Without asking, he poured four large and two small snifters of brandy. Handing both Faith and Henrietta one of the smaller ones, he murmured, 'I believe this can quite legitimately be considered an emergency,' in a dry undertone.

Naturally both the Reverend and Dougal were more than happy to indulge in a little restorative, with the worryingly silent Scot even smacking his lips. Flossy too made her partiality to a spot of brandy quite clear – her only uncertainty appeared to be which lap to beg in front of.

'So, what do you think our course of action should be?' Roan asked, finally sitting back down after handing Rafe the last glass. His eyes never left those of the Frenchman as he spoke, daring Raphael to suggest they stand down and leave matters to the *authorities*.

But Rafe had no intention of bringing in further outside assistance. Unbeknown to his listeners, his speech was as much an internal clarification of the current situation and by the time he reached the end, he'd recognised that these people were almost the only ones he could trust – although he had to wonder about the strange Scot who was now busy eying the bottom of his brandy glass mournfully.

'I think firstly we confirm Tristan is truly Philippe Montclair's son and heir,' he stated at length. 'Once it is proven and acknowledged by the wider public, it will be much more difficult for the conspirators to rid themselves of him. To do that, we need to go to France.'

'But what if you can't prove it?' Henrietta asked. 'Would he not be better to continue to live as Tristan Bernart?'

Rafe looked properly at her for the first time since he'd entered the room. His eyes were unexpectedly compassionate, and Henri swallowed a sudden lump, guessing what he was about to say.

'I do not think that's an option,' he responded. 'As you say in England, *the cat is out of the bag* now. It will not take long for those in charge to put two and two together. Once they realise the lost heir is still alive, they will take steps to silence him – this time forever.'

'But what if there is no ongoing conspiracy? What if Etienne Babin was simply the head of a group he created due to a deep-rooted hatred of the English?' Roan countered. 'At the end of the day, he had no idea of Tris's real identity.'

'You do not believe that any more than I do. Etienne Babin is a thug at heart, and my instinct is telling me that the man has been manipulated from the very beginning.' Rafe swallowed the rest of his brandy and shook his head. 'Are you a betting man Captain Carew? Are you willing to wager Tristan's life, and possibly the lives of members of your family that you are right and I am wrong?'

The silence was absolute until a sudden delighted chuckle. 'Tatties o'wer the side an' nae mistake,' Dougal crowed when all eyes turned towards him. 'Ah niver kenned for one wee minute we'd be sailing tae France, Augustus. So then, when are we off?'

Five

Augustus Shackleford was hard pushed to argue with Dougal's assessment of the situation. The *tatties* were indeed over the side, and worse, against all the odds, they would *all* be going to France. In truth, he'd have wagered the weekly collection money that the hardheaded Frenchman would throw out any suggestion that they make a jaunt of it. But Faith's argument that a group of men turning up at Montclair snooping around and asking questions would attract far more suspicion than a mixed company of people enjoying a short tour of the area unexpectedly won Augustin's support.

The Reverend was currently sitting by a cheerful fire in the small library after covertly helping himself to a second brandy from his son-in-law's excellent selection. Flossy was snoring happily on his lap, and everyone else – as far as he was aware – was getting ready for dinner. Staring into the fire the clergyman wondered for the umpteenth time at the Almighty's decidedly capricious sense of humour. There had been a time when he'd felt confident in every action - convinced God was directing his every move. But in recent years, he often felt plagued by indecision.

Solving mysteries had always been irresistible to him, but lately he found himself far more focused on the risks rather than the rewards. The Reverend sighed. Likely, it was simply his age. But he certainly wasn't ready to settle into a comfortable dotage with Agnes. When he really thought about it, there wasn't much that was *comfortable* about his wife. He'd got to the point where he was reluctant to admit to having a deuced cold, in case she accidentally poisoned him with one of her *medicines*. Faith was right, he really did need to remove all her potions and tinctures. Living at the Vicarage was becoming a test of fortitude...

Taking a sip of his brandy, he forced his mind back to the problem at hand. When the fictitious *tour* was first proposed, he'd imagined they would sail before Percy and Finn arrived. However, that was looking increasingly unlikely since Roan had sent urgent messages to Nicholas, Gabriel and Tristan asking that they attend him at Redstone House without delay. Naturally, there was no further explanation, in case any of the letters should fall into the wrong hands. Unfortunately, *without delay* could mean anything from a week to a month depending on how quickly the missives actually got into the *right* hands.

All in all, Augustus Shackleford was in a bit of a quandary. He did not dare send a note to Percy, since instructing his curate not to come without saying why was likely to bring the mutton-head running all the quicker.

The Reverend took another sip. The main problem was that nobody actually *knew* he'd invited Percy and Finn to Torquay. As soon as Finn set foot in the door and discovered they were *sailing to France*, there would be absolutely no way to avoid bringing him along short of locking him up – and even then, the boy was a passable lock picker courtesy of his 'Aunt' Patience. He was also more than capable of stowing away if he had to.

Which meant he and Percy would have to come as well.

Thunder and turf, the whole mission was beginning to look more like a deuced family outing by the minute, and he didn't imagine Raphael Augustin had quite this level of realism in mind when he agreed to the added passengers.

And then there was Dougal...

The thought of minding the unpredictable Scot on a sea voyage made him bilious. Of course, he could always simply return the troublemaker to Blackmore, but there was no more chance of Dougal agreeing to miss out on a sea voyage than there was Finn. That said, the thought of them both on deck at the same time filled him with horror. What were the odds of at least one of them falling overboard? Emitting a small involuntary moan, Reverend Shackleford quickly swallowed the rest of his brandy, hoping to erase the picture in his head. Finally, with another, longer sigh, he stared into the fire and allowed his mind to drift back to all the havey-cavey situations he and Percy had been involved in over the years. They'd put a rub in the way of many a varmint's plans. He gave a low chuckle, beginning to feel a little better. At least it would be a bit like the old times with Percy along.

And when all was said and done, it wasn't beyond the realm of possibility that he'd rediscover a bit of his old bottle. Not that there was much chance of Percy suddenly developing a backbone, since the chucklehead had never had one in the twenty-odd years he'd known him. However, Reverend Shackleford was certain that the curate would, like always, at least keep him company while he dusted down his superior investigative skills to prove that Tristan Bernart really was the Marquis de Montclair rather than the upstart currently lording it up in the chateau.

And they could always tie Dougal up.

~

The next few days were a hive of activity as both Roan and Faith began preparing for their upcoming trip. The only two members of the family who wouldn't be accompanying them were Joshua and Emma. Josh had mercifully returned to school a week earlier, and Emma was deemed too young. Though undeniably miffed at missing out, the youngest Carew was mollified at the thought of possibly staying at Blackmore for the duration.

Roan was out of the house more than he was in it as he sought to finish the repairs to his ship – the *Faith and Fortune*. It had indeed been fortunate that the vessel was not due to sail until January - though her First Mate, a taciturn man of middle age, was not best pleased at the idea of an impromptu trip to France.

Henrietta's offer of help was waved away by her mother who requested only that she see to her own packing – making sure to include warm, *sensible* clothing before drily reminding her daughter that rural Brittany was most definitely not Paris.

By the end of the week, Henri's trunk was closed and ready to be loaded onto the ship. More than anything, she wanted to erase the incident at the Poulton's Hotel, and by focusing on her packing, she was able to push the entire episode to the very back of her mind – most of the time anyway. Unfortunately, being busy did nothing to expunge the *feeling* of being seated in Raphael Augustin's lap. Indeed, she could vividly remember every embarrassing second, especially the incredible warmth of his body, the icy blue of his eyes, inches from her startled ones – moving from surprise to... something else. The feel of her heart hammering under his fingers as he instinctively sought to steady her.

In truth, she was entirely bewildered by the muddle of feelings the incident had provoked, and when the Frenchman announced he was returning to London while they were waiting for the arrival of the others, she didn't know whether to be relieved or sorry. He'd cited the need to research everything he could about the so-called caretaker currently residing in Chateau Montclair, without raising any undue suspicion. Unsurprisingly, no one could find fault with his reasoning.

Indeed, Henri suspected the entire household was actually grateful to see the back of the enigma that was Raphael Augustin, especially given his answer when questioned what would happen if Tristan categorically did not wish to pursue his claim.

The King's spy had merely shrugged and replied shortly that the matter was now out of his countryman's hands. He would be going to Montclair whether Tristan wished it or not.

Over the next few days, the weather became decidedly colder and drier, making it much easier to navigate the town on foot.

Reverend Shackleford was not normally prone to excessive introspection, but for some reason the possible presence of Percy had become an almost biblical catastrophe in his head. He didn't know where such an absurd feeling of imminent doom had come from and, after lying awake for two nights, put it down to eating too much cheese at dinner. Still, moping around Redstone House was certainly not helping matters, so he took it upon himself to show Dougal 'the sights' of Torquay. While he would rather have wandered the paths and lanes alone with only Flossy for company, he decided that Dougal left to his own devices was infinitely worse that having the mutton-head under his feet.

Fortunately, on their first perambulation, Henrietta happened to be coming out of the library and, on being informed of his intention, offered her company.

Almost immediately, Augustus Shackleford breathed a sigh of relief as his granddaughter chatted happily to Dougal, pointing out the seaside town's more interesting sights, leaving him to loiter behind with the excuse that Flossy needed to do her business. However, after ten minutes or so, the Reverend became interested despite himself. The town had changed quite considerably since his last visit – especially the harbour area, which now sported a charming promenade along the seafront.

As they walked, Henri pointed out her father's ship rocking gently at anchor a few yards from the shore. Even from here, the Reverend could tell the *Faith and Fortune* was bustling with activity. Sailors were swarming all over her rigging while provisions were being hauled up onto the deck.

'She's no wee lassy, that's fer sure,' Dougal declared excitedly as he stared over at the ship. 'Ah cannae wait tae climb aboard. Dae ye reckon yer da'll gie me the helm?'

Both his companions stared wordlessly at the enthusiastic Scot. Privately, Henrietta thought there was more chance of her father allowing Flossy behind the wheel, but she was too polite to say so. Her grandfather, on the other hand, had no such sensibilities and bluntly told Dougal to feel free to ask, providing he could swim.

Things very quickly went rapidly downhill from there, and as they began to attract attention, Henrietta frantically looked round for some sort of diversion. After a few seconds, she realised they were across the road from the Poulton's Hotel. Recollecting that the hotel had served a rather agreeable plate of biscuits on her last visit - and since Raphael Augustin was still in London as far as she was aware - Henri quickly proposed they take advantage of the hotel's proximity to enjoy an impromptu afternoon tea.

Fortunately, her suggestion put an end to the burgeoning quarrel, and five minutes later the three of them were enjoying the warmth of the Hotel's tearoom after being seated by a large picture window, which took delightful advantage of the agreeable view over the harbour.

Thinking of her last visit, Henrietta couldn't help looking round a little nervously, though whether that was on the off chance that the King's agent had returned to Torquay or the thought that somebody present may have been witness to her earlier faux pas. As her eyes travelled round the genteel room, her glance alighted on a table situated not six feet away. On it were sat two gentlemen leaning close to one another in earnest conversation.

She couldn't have said what it was about them that drew her attention, but whatever the reason, she found herself surreptitiously watching and listening as they waited for their tea. At first, she was unable to make out any words at all, but as her ears became more attuned to their murmured voices, she suddenly realised that one of them definitely wasn't English.

Frowning, she turned her chair slightly towards their table. In truth, foreigners were not all that uncommon in Torquay, but this man's accent, while a lot thicker than Raphael Augustin's, was not entirely dissimilar. Allowing her companions' conversation to flow over her head, Henri concentrated on the voices coming from her right and, seconds later, her heart jumped into her mouth as she heard a name she'd only heard recently.

Montclair.

Six

Rafe rubbed his forehead wearily, which did nothing to alleviate the throbbing over his right eye. He'd been searching through documents for the better part of the day, but the only success he'd had was a name - Claude Fontaine. The man had seemingly appeared out of nowhere in August 1808, claiming distant kinship to the murdered Marquis. He'd set himself up as caretaker of the Montclair estate and, as far as anyone knew, had lived quietly in the chateau ever since.

Raphael sat back in his chair, his lips pressing into a thin line. According to the report, after Fontaine's arrival, an agent of the Crown had remained in the area to keep a close watch on the self-appointed custodian for a full six months but had observed nothing to arouse suspicion. There had been no investigation into the man's background.

He thought back to his father's comments about Philippe de Montclair. The two men had remained good friends despite the distance between them, and Rafe well remembered how distressed his father's had been when the news of the Marquis's murder reached him.

Frowning, Raphael had a sudden thought. After they'd left France, Etienne Augustin had maintained a diary right up until his death in 1817, confessing to his son that it helped alleviate his guilt at abandoning the country of his birth. The box of diaries had been left to Raphael by his mother on her passing a mere twelve months later.

Though Rafe had never admitted it, reading his father's words had always been simply too painful, and it had been far easier to leave the diaries to gather dust in the box they'd arrived in. Out of sight and out of mind...

Sighing, he climbed ruefully to his feet. Maudlin sentimentality wasn't high on the list of traits a ruthless intelligence agent would readily admit to, and it was one Raphael had determinedly quashed during his long career. But then, neither was stupidity – and stubbornly ignoring a possibly valuable source of intelligence was exactly that. Grimacing, Rafe shook his head. His father's diaries had been left untouched for too long. Some bloody spy he was.

A half an hour later the diaries were piled on his desk in order of date while he helped himself to a brandy.

Reading his father's meanderings was as painful as Raphael had imagined, but what he hadn't bargained for was how *comforting* it was. It felt as though his father was in the room, and for the first time in years, the hardened spy felt actual tears gather at the back of his eyes.

To his relief there wasn't anything to either threaten or serve national security within their pages and Rafe allowed relief to swamp him. He had no idea what he'd have done if something of vital importance had remained concealed due to foolish sentimentality. Losing his job would have been the least of it.

However, just as he was about to close the penultimate journal, a folded piece of paper slipped out from between the pages and dropped onto the floor. Frowning, he bent down and picked it up. Unfolding the paper, he quickly realised it was a letter. Seconds later, his heart slammed in his chest as he read the informal signature.

Philippe.

Straining, Henrietta did her best to hear the conversation, but despite her focus, she was only able to make out the odd word. She wanted to scream in frustration. Then, just as she was about to give up, she heard the name of her father's ship. The words *Faith and Fortune* were followed by, 'Oui, he is onboard.'

Who was onboard?

Henri was so focused on the table next to them that she didn't initially register the arrival of their tea, and she jumped when her grandfather tapped her on the shoulder. 'A penny for your thoughts,' he quizzed her, his eyebrows raised in enquiry. As he spoke the two men were climbing to their feet and Henrietta wanted to cry. Helplessly she watched them go, the tea remaining in the teapot in front of her.

'Is something the matter, girl, you look as queer as Dick's hatband?' her grandfather commented gruffly as she finally lifted the teapot.

With trembling hands, Henrietta poured out the tea. As she handed the cups over, a large plate of biscuits arrived, much to Dougal's delight. Helping himself to a wafer, the Scot patted her kindly on the arm. 'Dinnae fash yerself, lass,' he murmured spraying bits of wafer everywhere, 'Ah ken a biscuit'll put ye tae rights.' He held out the plate, completely oblivious to the pieces of wafer now decorating her bodice.

'I think those two men were talking about my father's ship,' she whispered after making sure the objects of her attention were gone.

Her grandfather frowned. 'What were they saying?'

'I couldn't hear exactly, but I know they mentioned *Faith and Fortune*.'

Dougal shrugged. 'It be a bonny ship, lass,' he commented, helping himself to another wafer.

'You don't understand,' Henri answered fearfully, 'I think one of them was French.' She paused as her two companions stared at her. 'He said, *Oui, he's onboard*.'

'Thunder an' turf,' the Reverend breathed, we've got a Froggie spy sailing with us.'

'We dinnae ken that fer sure,' Dougal protested, seeing his trip to France disappearing faster than he could say *Sassenach.*

'They also mentioned Montclair,' Henrietta interrupted. 'That's what caught my interest. I think we should tell my father.'

'Noo, just haud on, mebbe we need tae check the facts first,' Dougal countered hurriedly. 'Ah mean, gaun half-cocked an' accusin' random sailors o' bein' Froggies will nae gie us the bampot. Ah'm thinkin' we need tae come up wi' a plan.'

Henrietta looked askance at the Scot. 'I have a plan – to tell my father.'

Reverend Shackleford pursed his lips, wondering if Percy and Finn's imminent arrival could actually be divine intervention after all. He gave a self-conscious cough before declaring loudly, 'It's a shame Percy and Finn aren't here...'

'Grandfather, surely you...'

'...Aye, Finn's the lad we need,' Dougal enthused. 'We'll nae find better tae dae a spot o' lurkin' wi-oot giein the game away.'

'Surely you can't be...' Henrietta sputtered.

'... It's true, Finn's a dab hand at making himself invisible,' the Reverend agreed fervently. Suddenly his presentment of doom seemed much less... *doomlike.* He gave an enthusiastic nod for good measure, only to suddenly freeze suddenly as a small, familiar voice spoke up at his elbow.

'What we investigatin' Revren?' the small, familiar voice suddenly cut in. The three of them turned round to find themselves staring into the grinning face of Finn Noon. 'Hae ye got any tablet?'

Heart thudding, Raphael spread the missive out on the flat surface. It was badly creased, making some of the words difficult to read. Glancing over to the window, he realised that the light was almost gone – a whole afternoon had passed while he'd been engrossed in his father's words. Hurriedly rising from his chair, Rafe lit the candle already waiting on the desk and moved it closer to the cramped writing.

A minute or so later, he sat down heavily.

Philippe de Montclair had a bastard half-brother. His name was Claude Fontaine.

The letter spoke of the Marquis's initial joy at the discovery, his efforts to ensure that his half sibling received the best possible education, despite his illegitimacy. All was apparently well until Philippe's son Tristan was born. Soon after, Claude disappeared and despite extensive enquiries commissioned by the Marquis, he'd seemingly vanished into thin air.

The letter requested that on the event of his death, Etienne was to make doubly sure that Claude Fontaine was given one thousand francs – the sum already written into the Marquis's will. As a bastard son, Claude could never inherit, even if there had been no legitimate heir, but Philippe wanted to ensure his brother was financially secure at the very least. The letter was signed and dated 5th March 1803. Below the signature was the official Montclair seal.

Raphael sat back in his chair, the pieces finally beginning to coalesce into a picture that made his blood run cold. The man posing as a distant cousin was in reality Philippe de Montclair's half-brother. It explained everything – his resemblance to the family, the refusal to claim the title, and most damning of all, the motive. He might never be able to inherit, but he could certainly steal what he believed should have been his by right.

And clearly Fontaine had known about young Tristan's existence all those years ago...

But what it didn't tell him was whether the attack on Montclair was purely for personal gain, or part of a larger conspiracy as he'd previously suspected.

And was the presence of Tristan in the same cell as d'Ansouis and Babin coincidence, or was he placed there deliberately?

Rafe's hand curled into a fist on the desk. Had Fontaine suspected all along that Tristan Montclair was alive and well? If so, they could well be sailing directly into a trap...

Flossy of course was over the moon at the unexpected arrival of her second love and threw herself into the boy's arms with reckless abandon. After laughing and kissing her soundly on the nose, Finn tucked her under his arm, and without waiting to be invited, used his other hand to noisily drag over another chair, completely oblivious to the disapproving stares directed at him from other patrons. Once the seat was situated to his satisfaction - as close to the plate of biscuits as possible – he placed Flossy onto his lap and solemnly asked the little dog whether she'd prefer a wafer or a piece of shortbread.

Finally recovering from his surprise, the Reverend immediately looked round for Percy.

'Where the deuce is your father?' he asked when there seemed to be no sign of his curate.

'You didn't come from Blackmore all on your own, did you?' Henrietta was horrified.

'Ah wouldnae be surprised,' chortled Dougal. 'The lad's nae a feardie Sassenach.'

'Da's bin lookin' fer ye, Revren,' Finn announced, helping himself to two biscuits in each hand. 'An' ah reckon he be fair fizzin wi ye.' His voice dropped as he declared the last sentence and he looked furtively round the room as though expecting his father to pop out from behind a curtain.

'Tare an' hounds, he's not been chasing you since Blackmore, has he?' The Reverend Shackleford muttered, wondering if he was going to be in even more hot water when the angry curate finally caught up with him – though in all honesty, he couldn't imagine what had Percy so up in the boughs – after all, he hadn't been told anything yet.

'I think we need to tell your father where you are,' Henrietta stated firmly, 'He's probably worried sick.' She rose determinedly to her feet and pulled on her gloves. 'I expect you will wish to know why Finn believes his father is upset, Grandfather,' she continued briskly, eying her grandparent narrowly.

Augustus Shackleford stared back with an air of baffled innocence. In truth, he'd never wanted anything less, but at the end of the day, if this truly was the Almighty's plan, then the clergyman simply had to trust that He would inspire a suitable Canterbury tale to support it.

However, before they had chance to actually vacate the table, Percy Noon finally appeared at the door.

'Finn, how many times have I told you not to run off in a strange place,' he huffed loudly, drawing yet more unwanted stares from the surrounding tables – though it had to be said the looks were now a trifle more interested.

'Sorry, Da,' the boy answered cheerfully. 'But look, ah foond the Revren fer ye.'

'Percy! What a surprise,' Reverend Shackleford boomed, causing everyone within a hundred yards to jump.

The curate glared at his superior before turning his attention to Dougal. Suspecting he might well be looking for signs of demonic possession, Reverend Shackleford felt sweat begin to gather under his dog collar.

'An, Da,' Finn continued excitedly, before Percy had a chance to whip out his bottle of holy water, 'the Revren wants me tae dae a spot o' nosin around... On a *ship*.'

Seven

'I'm sorry, Grandpapa, I cannot possibly countenance keeping my father in the dark about something so important.' Henrietta firmly replaced her bonnet and turned to Percy. 'It is a pleasure as always to see you, Mr Noon,' she declared, 'even though it appears that no one actually knew you were coming.' She looked back at the Reverend and narrowed her eyes. 'Aside from my grandfather, I suspect.' She stepped away from the table with one last parting comment. 'I think you can safely assume that my father will wish to speak with you on your return, Grandpapa.'

And with that, she swept towards the entrance. 'Thunder an' turf, when the devil did she turn into such a deuced harpy?' Augustus Shackleford muttered as they watched her march up the street.

'Ah reckon the lass be all bum and parsley,' Dougal declared without much conviction.

'Well, since I have no idea what on earth Miss Carew is talking about, I am more than content to leave it to those that do,' Percy announced, before turning towards the Scot who was now arguing in heated whispers with Finn over the last biscuit. 'How are you feeling, Dougal?'

The Scot glanced up in surprise before snaking his hand out to snatch the biscuit while Finn was looking over at his father.

'Och, ye gaunnie nae dae that,' the boy protested indignantly as Dougal stuffed the entire wafer into his mouth.

Percy shook his head sadly, muttering, 'Gluttony, that's a definite sign.'

'Oh, for pity's sake, stubble it, Percy,' Reverend Shackleford retorted irritably, finally losing his temper with the whole sorry business. 'Dougal is no more possessed than you are.'

'What be possessed?' asked Finn, looking with interest at the elderly Scot's red face as he tried in vain to chew and swallow at the same time.

'Are you certain, Sir?' the curate responded doubtfully as Dougal began gasping for air.

'Ah reckon he be gaun tae boke,' Finn added helpfully.

Augustus Shackleford hurriedly climbed to his feet and began thumping the Scot's back. Seconds later, a large piece of wafer shot across the room.

In her never-ending search for the ultimate snack, Flossy instantly jumped off Finn's lap and immediately took a shortcut straight between the Reverend's legs, only to get hopelessly tangled in her master's cassock as her lead whipped round and tightened round the clergyman's left leg.

With a yell, the Reverend fell backwards with a whoomph onto Henrietta's vacated seat just as Flossy re-emerged into daylight. Seeing the piece of wafer mere yards away, the little dog put on one last burst of speed, dragging her captor straight off the chair to land at the feet of a waitress carrying a large tray of crumpets.

With a shriek, the serving girl fell over the Reverend's prone form. The tray she was holding flew towards the intended table with all the speed of a musket ball, where a rather buxom lady only narrowly missed being decapitated by a flying butter knife. As it was, the stuffed peacock on her bonnet looked livelier than it had ever been when it was still alive.

The whole debacle was over in seconds, but the resulting pandemonium looked likely to last for the rest of the day. Indeed, there was no guarantee that the Reverend would be able to get up off the floor before closing time.

Flossy, on the other hand, pounced on the piece of wafer with all the aplomb of a conquering hero, crunching triumphantly under a convenient table while completely ignoring the uproar around her...

Henrietta had hoped to speak with her father as soon as she got home, but on walking through the door, she was told that the Viscount and Viscountess Northwood had arrived in her absence, though sadly they were not accompanied by her cousins.

Sternly reminding herself that they were not preparing for a family outing, Henrietta hurried up to her bedchamber to remove her outer garments and make use of the chamber pot. Likely, both her parents were bringing their guests up to date. Should she interrupt?

In truth, Henri was torn. She was entirely certain that her father loved his family more than anything. But second to that came his crew – some of whom had even been with him on the *Albatross*. The information she possessed was important – of that she was certain, but if she blurted out what she'd heard and her father feared his crew in danger from a traitor, she was afraid he might be tempted to do something rash.

In the end, she remained in her bedchamber for the better part of an hour which just as well since it took It took most of that time for Gabriel Atwood to calm down – and that was mainly due to his wife's calm, pragmatic nature. Indeed, Henrietta would likely have been quite shocked to hear her uncle shout that he was breaking off the engagement and putting his daughter in a convent. Fortunately, her Aunt Hope managed to quell his rancour before the arrival of his prospective son-in-law by evenly pointing out that success in proving Tristan to be the legitimate heir to the Montclair title would at the very least secure

Roseanna's future. Her husband's muttered, 'Providing we all survive the attempt,' was roundly ignored.

Eventually, Henri could bear it no longer. Anxiety about sharing what she knew and wondering what was happening behind closed doors had her pacing her bedchamber floor until, finally, swearing under her breath, she wrenched open the door and stalked to the top of the stairs. She was just about to start her descent when the doorbell rang, and although she was unable to see who was on the other side, she could tell there was more than one person. Three steps down, she paused as their maid, Sarah, appeared to open the door.

On the other side stood her Uncle Nicholas, Tristan *Montclair* and Raphael Augustin.

To her complete and utter confusion, the sudden surge of relief flooding her only occurred *after* she caught sight of the King's chief intelligence officer...

Inexplicably reluctant to greet the latest guests, Henri retreated back up the stairs before she was spotted and watched from the shadows as the three men were taken immediately into the drawing room. Once the entrance hall was clear, she hurried downstairs, just as the front door opened again, this time to admit the Reverend, Percy, Finn and Dougal. To her alarm, her grandfather was leaning on Percy's arm. His pallor was that of a seven-day-old corpse – though, in fairness, she couldn't say for sure, since she'd never actually seen one.

Completely forgetting her earlier rancour towards him, she gasped. 'What on earth happened to you, Grandpapa? Have you been injured?'

'Ye'd be better tae ask that wee Jezebel doon there,' Dougal muttered darkly, nodding towards Flossy, who had the grace to look a little sheepish.

'It wasnae Flossy's fault,' countered Finn urgently as Henrietta helped Percy get the Reverend into the library. 'She jus' wanted the biscuit.'

With a frown, Henri sat her grandfather in a chair facing the fire before fetching a stool for him to rest his feet on. 'Can I get you anything,

Grandpapa?' she asked, suddenly afraid he might truly be at death's door. A long groan was her answer.

'Go and ask Sarah to bring some tea,' she told Finn, fear gripping her

A surprisingly strong hand gripped her arm. 'Never mind tea, I'll have a brandy,' the clergyman declared, before collapsing backwards and giving another, more theatrical groan.

Henrietta eyed him speculatively before turning to Percy. 'Is he truly hurt, Mr Noon?' she asked archly.

'I think it's his pride more than anything,' the curate retorted with a sigh, earning him a disgruntled look. 'Well, if we're being entirely truthful, Sir, if you really had any more than a few bruises, I'd be giving you the last rites.'

'I might still,' Augustus Shackleford muttered defensively. 'Tare an' hounds Percy, I'm beginning to think you're turning into a rusty guts. Look at how many times I've looked after you over the years? I mean all those bumps on the deuced head. To be honest, it's a wonder you're not addled.'

'Most of those bumps were as a result of being with you, Sir,' Percy responded tartly.

'What be addled?' asked Finn with interest. 'Be it a *bampot* like Dougal?'

'Ah'll hae ye ken ah be as sharp as if ah'd bin livin' on Glasgow mustard,' Dougal protested.

'*Brandy…*' The Reverend's groans were becoming ever more dramatic.

'If the priest is planning an imminent meeting with his maker, I think perhaps it would be a good plan to ensure he is not entirely foxed.' The dry voice sounded from the doorway.

'Chance would be a fine thing indeed,' Augustus Shackleford retorted, finally abandoning his *woe is me* rhetoric and sitting up.

Henrietta's face flamed at the sight of Raphael Augustin standing in the doorway.

'Is the meeting over?' she asked, proud of the evenness in her voice.

The agent shook his head as he advanced into the room. 'There are deliberations your family need to make without the presence of an outsider,' he stated with a shrug, 'and in truth, I cannot argue with your grandfather – there are occasions when only a large brandy will do.' He turned towards Percy. 'We have not yet been introduced, Sir, but may I pour you a glass?'

'Err, this is Percy Noon, Grandfather's curate,' Henrietta hurriedly interrupted, 'He's recently arrived with his son Finn.' She pointed at the boy, who saluted with a grin.

'So, laddie, ye giein' the thievin' Sassenachs the good stuff and leavin the rest o' us wi' *lemonade*?' Dougal questioned scornfully before Rafe could ask what the devil the curate and his son were doing here.

Gritting his teeth, Raphael turned his head to look at the eccentric Scot, eyebrows raised.

'Ah thought ye'd niver ask,' Dougal grinned, rubbing his hands together.

The agent returned to Percy, who coughed and murmured, 'It's a pleasure to make your acquaintance, Mr Augustin. I believe we missed one another at Blackmore. I have to admit it's been a very tiring day, and a brandy would be very welcome, thank you.'

To Henri's surprise, Raphael then turned to her. 'Even after so many years in your country, I still do not fully understand the etiquette that governs your society, so I will beg your forgiveness and ask anyway. May I pour you a small brandy, Miss Carew?'

Given the resulting flush of colour on her face, he might as well have asked if he could kiss her, and Henrietta was not unaware of the interested stares of the rest of the room, making matters much, much worse. 'I thank you, but no,' she managed after giving a small, embarrassed cough. The last thing she needed at this moment in time was to be half-sprung.

'It's actually fortuitous you turned up,' the Reverend declared, completely abandoning his *at death's door* stance once he had a brandy in his hand.

Raphael raised his eyebrows. 'How so?' he asked politely. 'Do you have something you wish to share, Reverend Shackleford?'

Henrietta glared at her grandfather while at the same time experiencing a sudden violent desire to box his ears. She knew exactly what he was about to say, and there was nothing she could do to stop him. Meanwhile, Percy looked bewildered, Dougal was practically hopping from one foot to another in anticipation, and Finn piped up helpfully, 'The Revren says ah be gaun tae *investigate*.'

'Investigate what, exactly?' the Frenchman quizzed, his tone deceptively mild.

Realising she had no choice, Henri favoured her bird-witted grandfather with one last hard stare and suggested they all sit down. Then, hesitantly at first, she told Raphael what she'd overheard at the Poulton's Hotel.

For a few seconds after she'd finished speaking, the Frenchman didn't say anything, and the room was silent aside from the noise generated by Finn as he bounced up and down in his chair.

'Was it your impression that these men knew about Tristan?' Raphael asked at length.

'I… I assumed they did,' Henrietta stuttered, surprised at the question.

'Assumption is the mother of many disasters,' the Frenchman retorted drily. 'Did you simply assume because you heard them mention the name Montclair?'

Henri opened her mouth to say yes, but then paused, thinking back to the scene. A second later, she closed her eyes in an effort to transport herself back to the tearoom and allowed her mind to replay the sequence of events. The name that attracted her attention was *Montclair*. The men spoke about her father's ship and finally, she heard them say that someone was onboard. Was there anything else - anything at all?

Frowning, she looked over at Raphael. 'I think I heard them mention a fountain. Does that mean anything to you?'

The agent's response was immediate. 'You're sure you heard that word – *fountain*?'

Henrietta nodded, alarmed. 'But it actually sounded more like *funtain*.'

'*Merde*,' Rafe swore softly and shook his head. 'I had hoped he would not yet know.

'This *Funtain* is a man?' queried the Reverend.

'Exactement,' Raphael retorted, reverting to French in his agitation. 'Claude Fontaine, to be precise. He is Tristan's uncle and the current steward of the Montclair estate.'

~

That the Duke of Blackmore's arrival coincided with that of the as yet unaware Marquis de Montclair was no accident. On receiving Roan's request, Tristan had actually returned to Blackmore to seek Nicholas's counsel before travelling on to Torquay together. Though neither had any idea why they'd been called urgently to Redstone House, both believed it had something to do with Raphael Augustin's suspicions concerning the *Revisionist* plot.

Neither had even considered that Tristan might prove to be heir to a title, and even the Duke's legendary aplomb slipped a little when Raphael broke the news.

Tristan, on the other hand, laughed out loud – until the agent showed him a small drawing of the murdered Marquis that had been printed in a newspaper at the time of the attack. Though the article itself was heavily censored in line with Napoleon Bonaparte's taste for propaganda at the time – even going as far as declaring the untimely murder a victory for the regime – there was no mistaking the resemblance.

Looking at Philippe de Montclair was like looking at Tristan.

Naturally, convincing Tristan of his real identity had only been the beginning of the debate. Raphael's decision to leave them to speak further without his presence was a calculated risk, but at the end of the day, he needed these people to trust him. He'd done himself no favours by his initial approach, but in fairness he hadn't suspected that he might find himself in a position where he dared trust no one in his network. Not to mention the fear that there might actually be someone high up in the British Government involved in a conspiracy he'd never even bloody well heard of.

Rafe directed his mind towards the information Henrietta had just given him. He hadn't yet revealed to anyone the information he'd discovered in his father's diaries, and the knowledge that Claude Fontaine could already be one step ahead of them made him want to cast up his account. Where had the *bâtard* learned about their plans to sail to France? In truth, it could only be through knowing his nephew was still alive... Raphael gritted his teeth. His fear that they were sailing into a trap increased a hundredfold.

Especially as he now knew that one of *Faith and For*tune's crew was a traitor.

Eight

When Roan came looking for Raphael, he didn't hide either his surprise or his suspicion on discovering the Frenchman with his father-in-law and daughter - and his wariness certainly didn't lesson when the agent immediately asked Henrietta to close the library door.

It was then that Roan caught sight of Percy and Finn. After the briefest of hesitations, he greeted them both warmly, though his welcome was followed with a *look* towards his father-in-law hinting at the *intimate* discussion they'd be having in the very near future. The Reverend's expression was that of a man who'd been caught with his hand in the collection box, though when Roan added, 'I'm certain Augustus will not object to sharing his bedchamber with you both since the house is currently full,' his expression swiftly went from shifty to horrified, causing Roan to chuckle inwardly.

Ignoring his father-in-law's sputtered objections, Roan turned towards Raphael and waited for the explanation he assumed would be forthcoming. The last thing he expected was for the Frenchman to suggest they postpone any further family discussion until the morrow, and he instinctively began shaking his head, however, on catching the Frenchman's sombre expression, he hesitated and frowned, before finally shrugging and nodding. 'You're right. Everyone is tired, and I think a little lighthearted conversation over dinner would benefit us all. You will stay, of course, Mr Augustin?'

Raphael nodded in turn, then after a slight pause, added, 'I believe that since we could well be risking our lives together, it is time for you to call me Rafe.' His voice was dry, but underneath, there was an uncertainty Roan hadn't heard from the Frenchman before.

The sea captain raised his eyebrows but bent his head in agreement before turning back to his beleaguered father-in-law and drily suggesting the Reverend take his guests to get settled in.

After smothering a half smile, Henrietta offered her help, while Finn bent down to pick up Flossy saying, 'Ye ken that, lass, we goan tae be sleeping together – all o' us.' Augustus Shackleford looked about to cry as the procession made its way to the door.

As Roan made to follow them, intending to inform the rest of the family of their decision - and his wife of their unexpected additional guests, Raphael held him back, requesting in an undertone that they hold a quiet meeting once the rest of the household had retired. After favouring the agent with a hard stare, Roan acquiesced before suggesting that in addition to the two of them, they invite Nicholas, Tristan and Gabriel. Forcing down an unaccustomed awkwardness at hearing the men's given names, even though he himself had invited the casual intimacy, Rafe agreed.

In truth, Raphael had avoided getting too close to people throughout the whole of his adult life. It was infinitely easier to hold them at a distance and thus avoid potentially messy complications.

Such as an unexpected attraction to the daughter of the house...

With an inward grimace, Rafe suggested that the best way to instigate the meeting would be for Roan to casually propose one last glass of port before bed to the other three men...

Henrietta sat on her bed, staring into her open wardrobe. She was accustomed to spending very little time on deciding what to wear for dinner, generally alternating between a serviceable blue dress with a silver sash and an equally serviceable brown dress with a gold sash. If she suddenly appeared downstairs in one of her three special-occasion dresses, Henri knew her parents would notice immediately.

And it wasn't their attention she wished to attract.

Raphael Augustin. She murmured his name out loud, testing the sound of it on her tongue. Of course, she could tell herself that her attraction was merely because so few men crossed her path. Indeed, the last man to show any interest in her had been a solicitor her father's age. Henri shuddered, thinking back to his straining waistcoat and sweaty forehead.

Perhaps it was the fact that the King's agent was French. She couldn't deny she'd initially found Tristan very attractive – even lamenting that Roseanna had met him first. But on seeing her cousin's betrothed again this morning, she'd felt nothing.

She dragged her thoughts back to what to wear for dinner. That neither of her parents would approve of her infatuation was certain, and the last thing she wanted to do was to draw the wrong kind of attention to herself by dressing in a gown she would normally save for visits to Blackmore. Sighing, she climbed to her feet and picked out the brown dress, which her mother always maintained brought out the warmth of her hazel eyes.

Pulling off her woollen day dress, she swapped over quickly. Despite a cheerful fire burning in the hearth, the bedchamber had not yet warmed up. The weather had changed from mild and damp to unusually cold within the space of hours, which was yet another reason to choose the brown dress since it had been sewn from heavy taffeta.

Pulling the pins out of her hair, Henri dragged a brush through it, bemoaning the fact that Eliza, their one and only lady's maid, was busy with her mother and Aunt Hope, leaving the younger women to style their own locks.

Grimacing at her reflection in the mirror, Henrietta went to pull open a drawer, intending to pick out her usual ribbon when all of a sudden something hit her bedchamber window. Startled, Henri almost dropped the candlestick she was holding. Seconds later, there was another cracking sound, and for a moment she thought the pane was broken. Holding the candle high, she stepped towards the window and parted the curtains, staring out into the dark. When the noise came the third time, she saw the stone as it ricocheted off the window.

Clearly someone was out there, but all she could see in the candlelight was her own reflection.

Hurriedly putting the candlestick back on the mantelpiece, she went back to the window and peered downwards. Seconds later, she drew in a disbelieving breath.

Standing below, shivering in the cold, was her cousin Roseanna.

With a muttered expletive, she dropped the curtains and hurried towards the door. Seconds later she was rushing down the stairs, only slowing down as she crossed the entrance hall. As soon as she reached the narrow inner hallway leading to the scullery and back door, she sped up again, trailing her hand against the wall to avoid stumbling in the dark.

Finally reaching the tradesman's door, she unlocked it with trembling fingers and wrenched it open, leaning forward to peer out into the night.

Seconds later, her cousin materialised out of the gloom, shivering uncontrollably. Without preamble, Henri yanked her inside, whispering heatedly, 'What the devil are you doing here, Rosie? *How* did you get here?'

Roseanna shook her head, clearly unable to frame a coherent sentence, and, forcing down her panic, Henrietta shut and locked the door, then as swiftly as she could, guided her cousin back towards the main part of the house. This time, instead of heading out into the entrance hall and up the main staircase, she turned towards the little-used back servants' stairs. A couple of minutes later, after checking the coast was clear, she dragged her cousin into her bedchamber.

Seating Rosie in a small chair close to the fire, Henrietta dragged the heavy coverlet off the bed and wrapped it round her cousin's still-shaking shoulders, finally kneeling down at her feet.

'How did you get here, Rosie?' she asked again, looking up into her cousin's pale features.

'I came on the stagecoach with Doris,' Roseanna stammered after a few seconds.

Henrietta sat back on her heels and shook her head. 'How on earth did you persuade your mother's maid to do such a thing?' she breathed. 'Doris could lose her position for this.'

'She was visiting her family in Paignton, and I told her I'd travel on my own if she refused to allow me to accompany her,' Rosie retorted wearily, laying her head back against the back of the chair.

Henri grimaced in disbelief. 'Did you tell Frankie what you were going to do?' she asked.

'She's staying at Ravenstone,' Roseanna returned. 'Mother and Father stopped overnight to break their journey here.'

'Surely they wanted you to go with her?'

'Of course,' Rosie answered, 'but once I knew Uncle Roan had invited Tristan and Uncle Nicholas to Torquay, I was afraid something terrible had happened.' She leaned forward and took Henrietta's hand. 'Please don't give me away, Henri. I'll stay here in your chamber – you won't know I'm here...'

'And what about Tristan?' Henrietta quizzed her. 'What will he do when he finds out you're here?'

Roseanna's expression turned mulish. It was so incongruous on her usually affable, *wouldn't say boo to a goose* cousin that Henrietta actually laughed, much to her impromptu guest's chagrin. Henri took a deep breath and continued, 'I think I need to explain everything that's happened sweet. And then you really need do to speak with Tristan...'

By unspoken consent, the conversation during dinner avoided the subject of unexpected inheritances and murderous conspiracies – not least because of the unexpected addition of impressionable nine-year-old ears at the table.

Naturally, Tristan was very subdued, and Henrietta could only imagine how difficult it must have been for him to accept the bizarre turn of events. Indeed, there was every chance he still hadn't entirely absorbed what most people would assume was nothing more than a bag of moonshine. And not only that, but to discover the names of his parents in one breath and be told they'd been murdered in the second would give anybody a fit of the blue devils, even if it did make him a marquis.

Whatever other ramifications might come from Roseanna's arrival, Henri knew that Tristan at least was going to be very glad to see his betrothed. Unfortunately, she hadn't quite worked out how that was going to happen without alerting the whole household, especially if she was to avoid utterly ruining either her or Rosie's reputation while she was at it. Clearly, she'd not inherited her grandfather's propensity to come up with a Banbury story at the drop of a hat...

A loud slurping sound brought out of her reverie, and glancing to her left she realised that Finn practically had his head in his soup bowl as he attempted to get as much onto the spoon and then into his mouth as possible, only slowing down after his father laid a hand lightly on his arm.

Chuckling inwardly, she took a sip of her own soup, just as a sudden thought assailed her. Should she bring her grandfather in on the secret? He was a man of the cloth after all and could feasibly provide an acceptable chaperone during any tête-à-tête, thus saving everyone's reputation.

It would also be much easier for him to take Tristan aside and tell him of Rosie's arrival, as well as convince the Frenchman *not* to do the honourable thing by telling Rosie's father. All she had to do was find an opportunity to speak privately with the Reverend while avoiding the eagle eyes of her parents...

Henrietta took another sip, her thoughts falling over each other. Truly, the whole situation was becoming ridiculously complicated. How on earth Raphael handled this kind of havey cavey business all the time, she had no idea.

Thinking about the King's agent, she automatically lifted her eyes, seeking him out, just as his head turned towards her. For a few heart-stopping seconds, he stared at her with an intensity that should have sent her running, but instead, she experienced a totally unfamiliar sensation deep in her core, which had her fighting the urge to squirm in her chair. With the inevitable blush creeping up her neck, she swiftly looked down. Her heart was beating as though it wanted to escape from her chest, and she found herself taking small, panting breaths. What the devil was wrong with her? No man *had ever* caused her body to react so.

Did Roseanna feel the same way when she looked at Tristan. What about her other cousins - Jennifer and Mercedes? Hurriedly, Henrietta picked up her spoon and concentrated on finishing her soup, allowing the conversation to flow over her.

She was entirely aware that allowing herself to feel anything for Raphael Augustin was foolish in the extreme. He was not in the market for a wife. Indeed, she doubted he had any intention of leg-shackling himself to anybody, let alone a woman barely out of the schoolroom. The feelings she was experiencing were merely infatuation. She'd never met anyone like him before, and she was certain that was the reason for her strong attraction.

What about the way he looks at you? the small voice in her head argued.

Henri gritted her teeth. Now really was not the time for soul-searching. Determinedly, she favoured the maid with a bright smile as the young woman took away the empty soup bowl.

'Ah niver in all ma days seed such a braw sight,' an awe-stricken voice breathed beside her. Turning to Finn, she saw him staring in wonder at the steak and kidney pie now steaming on the plate in front of him. The boy looked to be almost in tears. 'Ah reckon ah be deid and gaun tae heaven,' he murmured, picking up his fork and holding it like a shovel. Over his head, Henrietta smiled encouragingly at Percy, who was sighing through gritted teeth as he tried in vain to get Finn to use the knife without looking as though he was about to stab someone.

As she tucked into her own pie, Henri vowed to take a leaf out of Finn's book. If she was going to get excited about anything, much better for it to be food...

Nine

The news that Tristan was almost certainly the heir to an old and distinguished French title had in truth not come as a complete surprise to Nicholas Sinclair.

And as he sat listening to Raphael Augustin explain his reasons for believing there to be a link between the *Revisionists* and Montclair, the Duke had never felt so angry – with himself.

The simple fact of the matter was that he'd wanted the whole bloody conspiracy tied up neatly even though he knew in his heart of hearts that nothing was ever that simple.

If the King's agent had not recognised Tristan, who knew what mischief those hiding in the shadows might have gone on to perpetrate – and still might yet do so.

Nicholas was sitting in the library with Raphael, Roan, Gabriel and Tristan, purportedly for the last glass of port before bed as the agent had proposed earlier. That had been a couple of hours ago now, and Rafe had gone through everything he knew, everything he believed, and everything he feared, touching lastly on the possibility that there might be a traitor onboard the *Faith and Fortune*.

'So, you think this Claude Fontaine knows that his nephew is alive and well and believes he is coming to claim his inheritance?' Nicholas clarified.

Raphael nodded. 'If I was a betting man, I would wager he's been looking for Tristan for a long time.'

'Why the bloody hell didn't I choose another name?' Tristan grated. 'I only picked Tristan because I liked it, not because I believed it was mine.'

'It's possible that some part of you recognised it as yours,' Raphael answered with a shrug.

'But even if Fontaine *has* been searching, how can we be sure that he found me?' Tris interjected harshly.

'We can't,' Rafe retorted. 'If you're looking for proof that your uncle knows about you, all we have is an overheard conversation and gut instinct.' He paused before adding carefully, 'My men are interrogating Babin as we speak and there is an outside chance he will give up Claude Fontaine's name, but, in truth, if there is someone higher up orchestrating things, they are unlikely to get even that much from him. In fact, there is a very good chance that Babin will not last the week.'

'Can you not have him moved?' Gabriel demanded. 'God knows I have no sympathy for the bastard, but he's the only solid lead we have.'

'If I do, it will simply alert whoever is behind this of our suspicions,' Raphael countered, his voice tight. 'And at this point in time I dare not trust anyone in my organisation.' He clenched his fists in frustration. 'Do not think I am condoning murder – even of an evil *bâtard* like Babin. But at the moment, I believe Fontaine is under the impression that his nephew simply wishes to reclaim his inheritance and remains ignorant of any Montclair connection to the *Revisionists*. I think he will seek to rid himself of Tristan before the world learns of the heir's existence so that he can keep the money flowing from the Montclair coffers.'

'What if we proclaim my existence to the world now? Surely that will make it infinitely more difficult for him to arrange a convenient accident,' Tristan intervened drily.

'If we do that, whoever is masterminding this conspiracy will retreat into the shadows and we may never discover their identity. Our best chance is to force Fontaine's hand – get him to overreach himself.'

'Using me as bait.' clarified Tristan.

Raphael nodded ruefully.

'Naturally the easiest solution would be to ensure Tris suffers a fatal accident at sea, before he even arrives at Montclair,' Roan commented. 'I have a number of crew only recently joined the *Fortune*, so it's possible one or more of them could be in Fontaine's pay.' He turned to Raphael. 'What do you propose we do to flush out any traitors on board?'

Raphael paused for a second before murmuring, 'I think we have an ideal person to poke around the ship without being noticed, in fact, he told me himself just how good he was at *snooping*.'

'*Finn*.' Nicholas verbalised what everyone else was thinking. 'I must confess I was taken aback to see him and Percy here. How the devil did that happen?'

'I have no idea,' Roan shrugged. 'Clearly, they were invited by Augustus – most likely to provide support with the menace that is Dougal Galbraith – though he's never likely to admit it. Still, Finn's presence is fortunate.'

'Surely we cannot sanction putting the boy in danger,' argued Tristan.

'Even I'm not callous enough to risk the boy's safety,' Rafe retorted drily. 'Since it is common knowledge that we sail in three days, I suggest you take Finn with you from tomorrow, Roan - with the excuse that he wishes to learn all about the ship. Undoubtedly, he will get underfoot on occasions, but much of the time he will be ignored and able to watch and listen unnoticed.'

'I think it unlikely our traitor will give himself away this late in the game,' countered Gabriel, 'not if he wishes to be in a convenient position to push Tristan overboard.'

'Helpful,' drawled Tristan.

'But what if our traitor receives new, *vital* information that he needs to share?' Rafe mooted. 'Something he deems so important he'll risk leaving the ship.'

There was a short silence, then Roan began to smile. 'The crew are waiting for confirmation of our final destination,' he declared. 'I had not decided whether to anchor off St. Malo in Solidor Bay, or Perros-Guirec. The latter is much closer to Lannion and Montclair – only one or two hours by carriage – but the water is much shallower.'

'Montclair is a two-day journey from Solidor Bay, depending on the weather. If Fontaine thinks we're sailing there, my guess is he'll be delighted. It will give him plenty of opportunity to ambush us before we get to Lannion,' Raphael asserted. 'He won't know whether his man has been successful in eliminating Tristan during the crossing, so it's reasonable to assume that he and his men will be waiting for us.'

'If you're going to feed him a Canturbury tale, it will need to be early enough to give our man enough time to pass the information on, and for Fontaine's collaborators in Torquay to get well ahead of us,' Nicholas stated, immediately getting his brother-in-law's drift.

'We'll leave with the afternoon tide three days hence,' Roan commented. 'If I make the announcement first thing the day after tomorrow, once we've moved the ship to the quayside for embarkation, that's a full day and a half before we're due to sail.'

'My guess is they'll have a small cutter,' mused Tristan, 'which should be more than capable of reaching Montclair before we actually sail. If the *Fortune* takes three days, Fontaine will be ready and waiting for us...'

'*In the wrong place,*' Gabriel grinned.

'Doubtless our man will try to slip away during the confusion of boarding,' Roan added, 'hopefully taking no notice of a small lad...'

Rafe nodded slowly. 'It will certainly work in our favour if we can get to Montclair while Fontaine is absent. Perhaps it will finally gain us the upper hand.'

'Speaking of upper hands,' Tristan interrupted. 'What exactly are our plans if you manage to deliver me to Montclair unscathed?'

Raphael grimaced. 'I'd like to say I have it all planned out,' he sighed. 'Unfortunately, that wouldn't be entirely accurate. It's my hope there will be someone still at Montclair who knew you as a boy – perhaps even fled with you to Pontorson. Once we get to Lannion, there will be no need to remain in hiding. In fact, my intention is to proclaim your arrival to all and sundry. The more people who hear about your return, the less likely it is that you'll suffer a quiet accident.

'Of course, we have to face the possibility that Fontaine may not take the bait and leave Montclair, and even if he *is* waiting to ambush us in St. Malo, he'll quickly realise he's been duped and return as quickly as possible. But by then, I'm hoping it will be too late for him to prevent the news of the Marquis's return from spreading.'

Rafe stopped and grimaced before adding, 'I freely admit that in the beginning I failed to anticipate the possibility that Claude Fontaine might be one step ahead of us, but the only thing I can say to reassure you gentlemen is that despite any evidence to the contrary, I am good at what I do.' He spoke entirely without conceit as he added, 'With your help, I *will* reinstate Tristan as the rightful Marquis de Montclair and expose the bastard who's been coordinating this whole bloody conspiracy since the beginning.'

'Very pretty speech,' Gabriel drawled without rancour.

Rafe spread his hands and shrugged. 'Naturally. I'm French...'

'I'll speak with my First Mate tomorrow morning,' Roan pronounced. 'We were both on *Albatross* together, and I'd trust him with my life – *have* done so on several occasions.' He stood up. 'It's late, gentlemen. I suggest we adjourn and continue our discussion after I've met with Mr Spalding.'

'I think we will have to include Augustus and Percy in our plans,' Nicholas interrupted with a sigh. 'As Finn's father, we cannot in all conscience exclude Percy, but unfortunately, that means the Reverend will also insist on being included.' The Duke gave a rueful shrug. 'Augustus might well be the most frustrating individual alive, but there's no denying he's better than most at shamming it when he's forced into a corner.' He looked over at Raphael and gave a dry chuckle. 'Mayhap you should think about recruiting him...'

'Forgive my lack of enthusiasm, your grace,' Rafe countered with a pained chuckle, 'but from what little I've seen of your father-in-law, following orders is not one of his strong suits. In fairness, I had actually assumed that he and the outlandish Scottish gentleman would be sailing with us.' He turned to Roan. 'Is the ship able to accommodate Mr Noon and his son also?'

Roan sighed and nodded. 'Though our ruse of a family trip to France is wasted if Fontaine is expecting us. Perhaps we'd be better to simply abandon the ploy.'

Rafe shook his head. 'He currently believes us entirely unaware of his duplicity and I would prefer we not enlighten him. The last thing we need is for him to realise we are playing a double game. But not only that, it will be far more difficult for someone to harm Tristan with so many people onboard.'

'And I'd like to see you try and talk Hope out of it,' Gabriel added. 'Please feel free to put your suggestion to her...' The Viscount left the sentence hanging.

'As much as I'd prefer to accompany you, I believe I will better serve by remaining in England,' the Duke interjected. 'I find it hard to believe there are no rumours swirling around London at all, and I have contacts in Westminster I can trust.' He paused before adding drily, 'And putting aside the knowledge that my wife too will certainly have my hide if I go to France without her, Grace and I are expected in Grosvenor Square at the end of this month. I can easily bring the visit forward without any undue suspicion.' He paused, then looked directly at Raphael, his expression chagrined.

'I believe I owe you an apology, Monsieur Augustin,' he said finally, stiffly. 'I can only say I am not usually quite so pigheaded...'

The sudden burst of laughter from both Roan and Gabriel cut him off. Nicholas raised his eyebrows before giving a rueful grin and adding drily, 'Clearly there are those who would disagree.'

'I think this calls for a celebratory brandy before we finally retire, Roan chuckled, climbing to his feet.

'What the devil are we celebrating?' Nicholas growled, his eyes narrowing.

'What, other than you admitting you were wrong, Nick? Why, nothing at all...'

'Dae ye gae me a bit more bed, Revren? Yer big toe be verra nearly up ma nose, and tae be honest, it be mingin''

'Well, since your deuced toes look like you could grow potatoes in between 'em, I wouldn't go casting stones,' the Reverend retorted, dragging up the blanket to cover the offending digits just under his chin. 'There might be a bit more room if Flossy got out from under the damned blanket.'

'She be keepin' me warm, Revren, seein' as ye an' Da be hoggin' the blanket an' ye willnae let me keep ma boots on.'

With a long-suffering sigh, Reverend Shackleford gave his curate a shove. 'Can't you move over a bit, Percy?'

'Sorry, Sir,' came the mumbled response, followed by a loud snore.

All was quiet for a few moments, and Augustus Shackleford finally began to drift off until suddenly a crunching sound broke the silence. 'What in blazes are you doing now?' He growled, sitting up.

'It be ma puddin'' Finn explained, sitting up in turn and holding out a biscuit. 'Dae ye want one, Revren? Ah hae plenty under ma pillow.'

The Reverend stared incredulously at the boy. 'You had a deuced pudding,' he growled. 'In fact, I think you had three.'

'Four,' corrected the boy. 'Mam says ah be gettin' right guid wi' ma numbers.'

'You can't possibly be hungry,' Reverend Shackleford went on, wondering what the devil he was doing arguing with a nine-year-old boy in the middle of the night. 'And you're getting crumbs in the bed.'

Finn shrugged. 'It be a wee biscuit is all,' he retorted. 'I dinnae care aboot a few crumbs. Better'n lyin' 'ere wi yer mingin' bunions up ma nose.'

The Reverend gritted his teeth and opened his mouth to tell the boy in no uncertain terms that this was his deuced bed, and he'd decide what would be eaten in it, but he was forestalled by a sudden knock on the door.

'Thunder an' turf, you've woken the whole household,' the clergyman hissed.

'Ah didnae dae anythin',' protested Finn as the knock came again.

Gritting his teeth, the Reverend climbed out of bed and, shivering at the sudden rush of cold round his nether regions, hurried to the door, his nightshirt flapping round his ankles. 'What time do you call thi…?' he started, pulling open the door, only to stop and stare incredulously at his granddaughter, Henrietta.

'Has something happened?' he asked immediately, fearing the worst.

'Be somebody deid?' Finn quizzed with ghoulish relish, coming to stand beside the Reverend. 'Or gaunae be deid?' he added hopefully as Henrietta began shaking her head.

'No, nobody's dead – not even a little bit as far as I'm aware,' Henri muttered before adding in an undertone, 'Not yet anyway.' She paused and looked around the deserted landing before leaning forward and whispering, 'Rosie's here.'

'Rosie who?' the Reverend asked after a second.

Henrietta looked at him askance. 'Roseanna – your granddaughter.'

'What the devil is she doing in Torquay? How did she get here?'

'She...' Henrietta stopped and shook her head. 'It would take too long to tell you. I need you to fetch Tristan.'

Her grandfather stared at her in disbelief. 'Are you addled, girl? I can't be fetching gentlemen for you to have a cosy chat with in the middle of the night.'

'It's not me, it's Rosie.'

'Oh well, that makes it alright then,' he scoffed sarcastically.

'Ah dinnae ken her da'll see it that way,' Finn interrupted doubtfully.

The Reverend and Henri glared at the frowning boy for a second, then Henrietta shook her head, gritting her teeth in exasperation. 'I daren't leave it until tomorrow. What if Uncle Gabriel finds out she's here?'

'Ah reckon he'll be fizzin,' Finn offered helpfully.

'*Shut up, Finn,*' chorused the other two in heated whispers.

Shaking his head, the Reverend stepped out onto the landing, muttering, 'Lord save me from foolish chits and jaw-me-dead boys.'

'What be jaw-me deid?' Finn quizzed, following at their heels.

'Someone who talks too much,' Augustus Shackleford threw over his shoulder.

Seconds later, they were standing outside a bedchamber door. 'How do you know this is the right one?' the Reverend asked.

'I don't - I thought you did?' Henrietta retorted. 'How am I supposed to know which room an unmarried gentleman is sleeping in?' They stared at each other. After a few seconds, Finn shook his head with a sigh and stepped between them muttering, '*tumshie heids,*' under his breath as he pushed open the door.

Ten

'Of course I didn't know it was your parents' room?' Henrietta declared as the two cousins sat dutifully in the breakfast room the following morning waiting for the inevitable lecture. Though breakfast wasn't due for another couple of hours, their respective fathers had ordered the two women and their grandfather to make themselves available at seven a.m. prompt. While they were still awaiting the arrival of the Reverend, the housekeeper, Mrs Bellamy, had very kindly stoked up the fire and brought them some tea and toast, declaring that no one should take a roasting on an empty stomach. Henrietta certainly couldn't argue with that.

'I'm merely not in the habit of searching for men's bedchambers in the middle of the night,' she continued, taking a thoughtful bite of her toast. 'Do you think we've got Grandpapa in serious trouble?'

Roseanna sighed. 'Grandfather thrives on serious trouble – he's never happier than when he's in the suds. Everyone knows that.'

'Yes, but none of this was his fault.'

'It wasn't yours either, Henri,' Rosie sighed. 'I'm the one who's made a mull of the whole thing. I should have simply knocked at the front door like any normal person. My mother would have understood. After all, it's not like she's never tied her garter in public.'

'Really? Aunt Hope has always seemed the most sensible of all the sisters – nothing like Aunt Tempy or Patience.'

'Papa's always said the quiet ones are the worst,' Roseanna admitted with a small grin, before leaning forward and adding, 'Mother and Father were actually locked together in a cellar by a perfectly horrid man. *Before* they were wed...'

'What, alone?' Henri didn't know whether to be intrigued or horrified.

'*Totally* alone,' Rosie confided. 'It's not something they talk about much, but I do know it was Mother's voice that saved them.' She took a sip of tea.

Intrigue definitely won out over horror. 'How?' Henrietta asked. 'Did she sing or something?'. To her surprise, Roseanna nearly choked on her tea. 'I can only assume that you've never heard my mother's singing voice...'

They were interrupted by their grandfather's arrival. 'Is that fresh?' he quizzed cheerfully, pointing to the teapot and helping himself to a piece of toast. Henrietta regarded him dubiously. He certainly didn't look Friday-faced.

'See what I mean?' Roseanna whispered, eyebrows raised.

'Have they let you see your Frenchman yet?' Augustus Shackleford went on, seating himself at the table.

Henrietta gave an embarrassed cough. 'I didn't realise it, but he's not actually staying in the house. He's lodging at the Poulton's Hotel with Mr Augustin.'

The Reverend favoured her with a disbelieving look and shook his head, but before he had the chance to comment, Roan and Gabriel entered the room. Directly behind them was Tristan.

The supposed roasting turned out to be more of a reproach than anything else, and there was no argument over whether Roseanna would accompany them other than they should both be ready to board the *Faith and Fortune* immediately after breakfast on the morrow.

Finally, after inviting their grandfather to accompany him into the study, Henri was drily ordered to attend her cousin in the library so that she could speak with her fiancé without damaging any reputations...

Delighted that Rosie was not to be sent home, Henrietta followed the couple into the library, seating herself to the side of the large picture window. Once there, she discreetly turned her chair, better to observe the garden, and occupied herself by watching two seagulls fight over a few crumbs of bread. After only five minutes, they flew off, squawking, leaving the unfinished breadcrumbs scattered in the grass.

In her experience, seagulls did not usually relinquish their prize quite so easily. Surprised, Henrietta leaned forward to see what had spooked them and caught sight of a man who'd clearly entered the garden via the back gate. As she watched, he casually sat down on a bench underneath a large cherry tree and pulled out a pipe. While the bench was placed to take advantage of the glorious view over the harbour, it was not easily visible from the house, and Henri suspected he'd chosen the location deliberately. Frowning, she leaned forward but was unable to get any more than a side view. However, from what she could see, the man was wearing a uniform the colours of the *Faith and Fortune*.

Clearly, he was waiting for someone, most likely her father – but why was he sitting outside rather than coming into the house? Whatever his reasons, the man didn't wait for long. A mere fifteen minutes later, he emptied his pipe and left the same way he'd arrived.

~

The rest of the day was chaotic as packing was finalised and trunks were loaded onto carts to be taken to the ship.

The Duke of Blackmore departed, taking Emma and Eliza with him. On hugging her youngest daughter, Faith had laughingly cautioned her not to become too accustomed to having her own lady's maid.

Henrietta and Roseanna spent the rest of the morning in the library, well away from the disorder, though Henri suspected her cousin was keeping a low profile in case her father should change his mind about allowing her to sail with them. Rosie was subdued as they played a game of snap, clearly desperately worried about Tristan. Although she was aware of the possibility that her fiancé might actually be the heir to a French title, Roseanna was no gold digger – her concerns were entirely for Tristan and the risk he was taking. In truth, she'd have much preferred to forget she'd ever heard the name Montclair.

Henri too felt restless and anxious, though initially she couldn't pinpoint the cause of it. After a cold lunch delivered to them in the library, Roseanna retired to their shared bedchamber to rest since neither of them had got much sleep the night before.

Once on her own, Henrietta tried to read but found herself unable to concentrate – until the sudden squawking of seagulls fighting outside finally explained what had been bothering her. *The unknown sailor in the garden.* While it wasn't that uncommon for members of Fortune's crew to come up to the house, the whole episode had made her uneasy. After mulling it over in her head for another half an hour, she finally decided to speak with her father.

Climbing to her feet, she went looking for him, only to find out a few minutes later that both her parents had gone into Torquay. Muttering under her breath about family members who leave the house without informing other family members, Henrietta wondered what she should do.

Of course, there was always her grandfather – he would undoubtedly have a theory or two. With a sigh, Henri went searching, only to discover that he, Percy and Dougal had gone with her father to show Finn around the ship. Her muttering became slightly more colourful.

By now Henrietta was feeling entirely overlooked, unconsidered and, quite frankly, unappreciated.

And it was beginning to get dark. Fifteen more minutes and walking alone down to the harbourside would be out of the question.

Gritting her teeth, Henrietta went to fetch her coat. Then, without telling anyone where she was going, slipped out of the front door. The sensible part of her knew she was being extremely childish by not informing anyone she was leaving the house. She was also well aware that her Aunt Hope would have welcomed her company in the drawing room now that most of the trunks had been taken...

Unfortunately, the path of *petulance* was not quite as easy to get off as it was to get on, and marching down the hill in the gathering dusk, Henri stubbornly nurtured her grievances, until by the time she reached the harbourside, the little voice in her head was telling her she was the most unfortunate person alive. The fact that she'd spent the whole walk completely oblivious to her surroundings did not occur to her until she realised she'd missed the turnoff to *Fortune's* wharf and was now standing on an unfamiliar, disturbingly *dark* quayside - completely alone.

Raucous laughter erupted from a nearby tavern – undoubtedly filled with dockworkers and sailors, and glancing round, Henri felt the first stirring of fear. While Torquay was on the whole a safe town, young ladies were not generally seen loitering around the seedier areas of the harbourside - unless they were of a particular kind, of course.

Biting her lip, Henrietta turned round and hurried back towards the main quayside. To her left, she could see her father's ship rocking at anchor just beyond the wharf as the wind changed direction with the tide.

'Lookin' to earn yersel' a bit o blunt, darlin'?' The drunken words came from her right. With a small scream, Henri swung towards the voice. Panic gripped her as her eyes initially struggled to pierce the gloom, then a second later she stepped backwards as a huge hulking form lurched out of the darkness. ''Ow much fer a kiss?' he slurred, taking a long swallow out of the tankard he was carrying. He followed his words with a loud belch and a grin revealing a mouth full of rotten teeth.

'Don't come any closer,' Henrietta stammered, thrusting out her arm as if that would somehow ward him off. She continued to back away, her heart beating like a sledgehammer in her chest. How could she have been such a deuced widgeon?

'Unless you're looking to end your sorry life as fish food, I suggest you do not come one step closer.' Another voice, this time wintery cold.

Panting now, Henrietta looked over her shoulder at the new speaker, and let out a sob of relief as she recognised Raphael.

But this was a Raphael she'd never seen before. He barely glanced at her except to ask if she'd been hurt. At her murmured denial, he returned his attention to the man standing three feet away, who was rapidly sobering up. 'I was jus' bein' friendly to the lady,' he protested, taking a step backwards and holding his hands up in a conciliatory gesture.

'She has no interest in the type of friendship you are offering,' Rafe bit out, without taking his eyes off the assailant.

The man was larger than Raphael by far, and Henrietta could tell the second he realised it too. With a sneer, the brute stepped forward, drawling, 'I think we should let the little lady decide that.'

Henri had no idea what happened next, except that a moment later her would-be attacker was rolling on the ground holding his stomach and moaning.

Eyes wide, she turned to Raphael, who looked barely winded. She just had time to notice that his eyes were like flint before he took hold of her hand and marched her towards the lighted area of the quay. He was walking so fast that Henri struggled to keep up with him. For a second, she didn't realise he was speaking, but eventually, his stony voice pierced the fog in her mind.

'What the devil did you think you were doing wandering around Torquay harbour at this time of night?'

'It's hardly night,' she protested, running to keep up with his long strides. 'I wanted to speak with my father.'

'I doubt he has the time for a conversation with a foolish chit who doesn't know when to stay out of harm's way,' Rafe retorted through gritted teeth.

'Err... excuse me one moment,' Henrietta snapped, yanking her hand from his, causing him to stop with a muttered oath. 'What qualifies you to decide whether I should or shouldn't speak with *my* father? Or indeed what I should speak to him *about*? The last time I checked, you certainly hadn't developed any divine attributes.'

Raphael stared at her as though she were some kind of rare species he'd never observed before.

'You could have been hurt – or worse,' he finally said at length. The censure in his voice was gone, replaced by... in truth, Henri wasn't quite sure. But the look in his eyes was unmistakable. *Fear.*

Abruptly, her heart slammed against her chest for an entirely different reason. The Frenchman had been terrified *for her.* She told herself it meant nothing. He'd have come to the rescue of any woman in her position – and been equally concerned for their welfare.

Biting her lip, she looked down towards her feet. She was well aware that she'd been above foolish, and not only that, she'd told herself a complete Banbury story on her way down to the harbour. She looked up at Raphael, who was now regarding her much as he would a wild animal he was seeking to preserve.

'I think I owe you an apology,' she murmured, looking anywhere but into his eyes. 'You are perfectly correct; my actions today have been those of a sulky child.' She gave a small sigh before continuing matter-of-factly, 'Will you believe me if I say that anxiety has turned me into the mutton-headed harpy you see before you.'

'Mutton-headed harpy?' Raphael raised his eyebrows at the term, and after a second, they both started to laugh. At length, shaking his head, Rafe held out his arm. 'Please allow me to escort you to the *Faith and Fortune*. I believe your father is still onboard.'

'That will not be necessary,' Henrietta answered. 'I merely wanted to share something that happened this morning.' In spite of her words, she took his arm and allowed him to walk her towards the main quay.

'Is it something I can help with?' he asked carefully. 'I was heading towards the ship to speak with your father myself.'

Henrietta glanced sideways at him. She was finding it difficult to concentrate on anything other than the feel of his hard warmth. Finally, with a grimace, she described what she'd seen that morning.

'It's probably not important,' she finished. 'It's just that when I saw a man wearing *Fortune's* colours, I thought it was strange he was waiting in the garden rather than coming into the house.'

'Would you recognise the man if you saw him again?' Rafe asked after a moment.

She pursed her lips for a second, then shrugged. 'I doubt it – I only saw a side view of his face. Why? Do you think it important?'

He didn't answer immediately, and when he finally spoke, his tone was carefully neutral. 'In truth, I'm not sure, but those men you overheard at the hotel were getting their information from somewhere. I suspect there might well be a traitor aboard your father's ship.'

Henri looked at him sharply. 'Most of the crew have been with the *Fortune* for years,' she protested.

'Not all of them,' he answered pointedly.

Henrietta gritted her teeth – the fact that she'd found the sailor's presence in the garden unsettling was what had brought her to this point, so how could she disregard Raphael's comment? Instead of dismissing the idea, she nodded thoughtfully, just as they reached the Poulton's Hotel, standing imposingly on the other side of the road. 'Would you permit me to walk you back to Redstone House?' he asked, to her surprise.

As much as Henrietta wanted to tell him she was perfectly capable of taking herself home without an escort, somehow the words stuck in her throat. The truth was that the incident had shaken her badly.

'Unless, of course, you would prefer me to have my carriage brought round from the hotel stables?'

Henrietta smiled and shook her head. 'Thank you, but the walk will undoubtedly do me good, and I would be grateful for the company - providing you can spare the time, of course.' She ignored the small voice in her head that told her the walk would also keep him with her for longer...

'I'll wait at the house to speak with your father. I doubt he'll be long - we all have an early start tomorrow.'

They subsided into a surprisingly companionable silence as they crossed the road and turned back in the direction of the harbour. After a few minutes, Raphael looked down at her thoughtfully, but her face was in shadow. Full dark had descended during the confrontation on the quayside, and the number of people abroad had decreased significantly along with the temperature.

A couple of minutes later, they reached the bottom of the steep hill leading to Redstone House, and as they began their ascent, Rafe finally spoke. 'Forgive me if I'm overstepping, Miss Carew,' he murmured, 'but I cannot not help noticing that you are unusually astute...' He paused and left the words, *for a foolish young woman,* hanging in the air. Nevertheless, Henrietta didn't miss the implication. Eyebrows raised in echo of his earlier expression; she couldn't help it – she burst out laughing.

'Have I said something amusing?' he quizzed her, trying to keep the testiness from his voice.

'If that is a compliment, Mr Augustin, I can only say that your technique most definitely needs work.'

'It was *not* a compliment,' he growled in response, 'it was simply an observation.'

'Ah,' she responded as they began walking again. 'What can I say? High accolade indeed from a man whose very life might well depend on *observation.*'

'More often than not,' he agreed, beginning to enjoy the conversation despite his initial irritation. '*Observation* is everything.'

'So, since I am particularly astute – your words,' Henrietta continued as they started up the hill, 'I can only assume you wish me to refine my burgeoning *observation* skills.' She favoured him with a mischievous grin. 'In other words, you wish me to cultivate my nosiness.'

His mouth quirked. 'Perceptive too, I see. Is there no end to your accomplishments, Miss Carew?'

She looked up at him, another quip on her tongue, only to fall silent as a sudden light illuminated his face. She was vaguely aware of the lamp-lighter continuing up the hill after lighting the streetlamp ahead of them, but the look in the Frenchman's eyes as he stared down at her stole her breath. She couldn't have spoken if her life had depended on it.

Without thinking, she turned her body just enough to face him, leaning closer as she instinctively sought the heat of his body. For a second, he didn't move, simply stared down at her, eyes almost glittering in the dancing light. Then, with an incoherent murmur, his hands slid upwards to grip her arms, and he crushed her to him, his lips coming down on hers.

A white-hot fear gripped her for the briefest moment, then, with a small moan, she surrendered, sinking into his heat as she'd wanted to do since he first walked into Redstone House.

Then all thought fled as his lips slanted across hers, his mouth setting fire to her nerve endings with every stroke of his tongue. Sensation shot through her, centred at the juncture of her thighs, where physical evidence of her need gathered even now. Unconsciously, she sought to relieve the pressure, grinding herself against his hardness and rubbing her peaking nipples against the exquisite roughness of his jacket. She had no idea what she was reaching for, just that it was *there*, and *there*...

Then, just as the sensations began to intensify, Rafe suddenly, *shockingly*, tore his mouth from hers, sliding his hands down to grip her hips, holding her still. With a muttered, '*Merde*,' he continued to hold her hips captive, bending forward to rest his forehead on hers.

'Pardonne-moi - forgive me,' he whispered raggedly.

Henrietta squeezed her eyes shut, mortification flooding through her. A tightness gathered in her throat, and for one horrifying second, she thought she was going to cry.

She felt him pull back and set her away from him, oh so gently, and she wanted to scream. Blindly, she started to turn away, wanting nothing more than to escape. In answer, he tightened his grip and for a second the fear returned. Opening her eyes she looked up at him in panic... and gasped.

His eyes revealed his regret, but not only that. They exposed a *longing* – fierce and unmistakable.

'I can offer you nothing at the moment, chérie,' he murmured, staring down at her. 'And I can make no promises that the future will be any different.' He closed his eyes briefly, and when he opened them again, she saw clearly for the first time just how much he was torn between his unwavering sense of duty and the desire to live a different life. 'All I ask is that you wait until this thing is done,' he finished hoarsely.

She stared back at him, swallowing the sudden lump in her throat - there now for a different reason. She sensed his pain, his isolation and, above all, his overwhelming desire for peace.

A peace she knew she could give him.

Hesitantly, she lifted her hand and cupped his cheek. 'I will wait as long as you wish me to.'

'Oy, you in trouble, miss?' They had entirely forgotten the lamplighter, who'd finished lighting the lamps to the top of the hill and was now on his way back down again.

With a mischievous grin, she turned round and gave a small curtsy. 'I am perfectly well, thank you, kind sir. I fear my husband is a trifle disguised and consequently a little befogged. We are minutes from home, however, where a large bucket of cold water is ready and waiting.' She ignored Raphael's incredulous look and, tucking her arm in his, urged him forward, murmuring, 'Come along dearest, not far now.' As they passed, she smiled at her would-be rescuer, who gave a bemused shrug before continuing down towards the harbour.

'He thinks you a light skirt,' Raphael declared flatly when they were out of hearing distance.

'Quite likely,' agreed Henri. 'But I doubt he would recognise me again in broad daylight, so no harm is done.'

'I should not have...' Rafe started but got no further as Henrietta stopped and shook her head.

'There is nothing more to say,' she declared bluntly, facing him. 'At the moment, our focus must be on the task at hand. What comes after...' She left the sentence unfinished and gave another smile, this time wistful. 'We will see.'

'Wise, as well as perceptive, observant and astute,' he declared drily.

'Don't forget nosy...'

Fifteen minutes later they arrived at Redstone House, and as Raphael pushed open the gate, Henrietta immediately felt the earlier, easy familiarity begin to slip away. Instead of the light-hearted teasing that had felt so natural, their approach to the front door felt awkward and stilted.

'I think perhaps it would be better if I speak with your father onboard the Fortune,' he suggested ruefully as they faced one another on the doorstep.

'Running already?' Henrietta quipped, then could have bitten out her tongue.

To her surprise, his lips quirked. 'I can assure you, Miss Carew, I have no intention of running anywhere. But your altercation with the lamplighter brought home the precariousness of your situation, and I do not wish to risk your reputation any more than I already have. In truth, I was not thinking straight when I offered to walk you home.'

'Neither was I,' Henri sighed after a moment. 'Clearly, I'm not quite as astute as you imagined.'

'Where matters of the heart are concerned, it's very difficult to be objective,' Raphael responded quietly, staring down at her.

'Very,' she repeated faintly, wondering if he was going to kiss her again.

Instead, he drew in a ragged breath. 'Speaking of astute,' he finally went on huskily, 'I don't believe we finished our conversation earlier.'

'No, I don't believe we did,' Henri answered, her own voice barely audible. 'What was it you wished to say?'

'I would very much appreciate it if you would keep your eyes and ears open, Miss Carew,' he murmured. 'Even the smallest of incidences can make a difference when put into context.'

'Especially when one is both astute and observant,' Henrietta returned with a quirk of her lips.

He bent his head in acknowledgement. 'My thoughts exactly. If you see the man again...'

'...I will provide you with everything from the colour of his eyes to his shoe size...'

'...And of course, his tailor...'

They stared at each other, the absurdity of their conversation abruptly knocking down the unexpected barrier.

'So, you wish me to be your eyes and ears, Mr Augustin,' Henrietta murmured at length. 'Will I receive a salary?'

At that, Rafe laughed out loud. 'God help me if you ever decide to become a spy, Miss Carew,' he chuckled. 'I suspect the rules of espionage might have to be rewritten...'

Eleven

Staring up at the canopy above his bed at three a.m., Rafe went over and over his interaction with Henrietta Carew. That kissing her was singularly the most foolish thing he'd ever done in his life was without question, but quite frankly, that wasn't his real quandary. No, the biggest issue with the whole bacon-brained business was that he didn't regret it. Not even for one second. And that scared the living daylights out of him.

For the first time in his life, Rafe was actually imagining having a home. Not simply a place to leave his few belongings, but somewhere he belonged, with... God help him... a *family* waiting for him.

How the hell did it happen? *When* had it happened? He thought back to the few days he spent at Blackmore. The chaotic, boisterous, *joyous* family gathering that had captivated him against his will. Watching them all together had prompted a longing so painful he'd immediately pushed it deep down inside – instead, behaving like an arrogant fool.

Since then, he'd struggled to summon the unemotional, aloof side of him that always settled over him like a shroud when he was on a mission. And he was nearly *always* on an assignment of some kind...

Before meeting Henrietta, Rafe had considered women merely as a means of gaining information, well aware that most found him attractive. In his experience, there were two types of *ladies*. Young, genteel innocents who thrilled at the hidden danger they sensed in him but were content to flirt within the safety of their gilded cages, and those who were older, wiser and wanted to experience firsthand the thrill of that hidden danger. Both were equally useful in his line of work.

But Henrietta was of neither type. That she'd been sheltered he had no doubt, but despite her incorrigible wit, there was no guile to her at all. Experience told him the attraction between them was mutual, but she hadn't tried to flirt with him. Perhaps it was due to the serious nature of their current situation, but in all honesty, he suspected it had simply never occurred to her to do so.

When he'd spotted her being accosted by the drunken thug, Raphael had wanted to kill the bastard. His ability to operate dispassionately in every and all situations had deserted him entirely.

And therein lay his biggest dilemma. Somehow, he had to put his burgeoning feelings for Henrietta aside and deal with the problem at hand. If he failed to reinstate Tristan and put an end to the *Revisionists* once and for all, Raphael feared he would never be free of all the subterfuge and secrets. Indeed, there was one particular secret he hadn't yet shared, and when his duplicity finally came out – as it was certain to do, he was almost certain that Henrietta would want nothing more to do with him...

~

Naturally, Henrietta said nothing about the day's unexpected turn of events. In actual fact, she didn't even mention she'd been out of the house, and if she was quiet over dinner, well, in truth, so was everyone else. Looking round the table, she suspected the reality of what they were about to do was uppermost in everyone's mind. Even the bickering between her grandfather and Dougal was confined to the occasional kick under the table.

Once everyone had retired to their respective bedchambers, she'd been tempted to confide in Roseanna, but in truth her feelings about the Frenchman were confused. The sensations she'd felt when he kissed her were like nothing she'd ever experienced before, so instead, she spent the entire night tossing and turning until Rosie had grumpily questioned whether the bed had bugs.

Raphael had asked her to wait until after the current situation was resolved, but Henrietta knew very well that it might never be solved at all. What would happen then? Would he walk away?

Would he be *allowed* to walk away? He was undoubtedly the keeper of a multitude of secrets. Could someone like that ever have a normal life?

Henri didn't have any of the answers, nor would she any time soon. Whether she wished it or no, her only option was to watch as she'd been asked to do and let things run their course and when it was over, pick up the pieces...

'I have to say I am disappointed in you, Sir.'

Reverend Shackleford looked over at his curate in surprise. 'What the deuce are you mumbling on about Percy?' he asked.

The three of them were the first to board the *Faith and Fortune,* having arrived bright and early for two reasons. Firstly, Finn had spent the entire previous day ingratiating himself with the crew, and naturally they wished to take advantage of the excellent relationship the boy had cultivated. Secondly, and arguably more importantly, one more second in the bed with Percy and Finn could well have resulted one or both of them leaving the room through the window... What made it worse was the knowledge that Dougal had his own bedchamber.

'I brought my son to Torquay under false pretences,' Percy continued firmly.

The Reverend sputtered in indignation. 'You can't deny the lad's been having a wonderful time,' he went on, waving towards Finn, who was running up and down the deck under the benevolent eye of the crew, being chased by Flossy.

'You asked me to come to Torquay because you were concerned about Dougal's immortal soul,' Percy insisted.

'Well, that's not qu...' Augustus Shackleford, only to stop as Percy held up his hand. 'You said you thought he was possessed.'

'Well, I...'

'...That you thought Finn might well benefit from coming face to face with the forces of evil.'

Reverend Shackleford winced.

'Now, I'll be the first to admit that Dougal Galbraith could make even a saint's entry into heaven uncertain,' Percy went on sternly, 'but I think we both know he is *not* possessed, Sir.'

'I don't think the forces of evil would give him house room,' the Reverend muttered under his breath. At the curate's sharp look, he gave a sigh and nodded. 'You're right, Percy, lad. Though I'm not proud of it, I can't deny I've been tempted to violence on more than one occasion when dealing with Dougal. However, I have to admit there's been no evidence to suggest that old Nick has any particular interest in the bampot's soul – and I can't say I blame him...'

'Then, why did you ask me to come?' Percy quizzed him crossly. 'I had to leave the parish in old Tom's hands, and the last time he took over, he had half the congregation stocking up for the Second Coming.

'I assume that you had no idea that Finn might be asked to investigate a *traitor* when you sent the missive?' The curate's voice had turned from cross to suspicious, and with a small cough, the Reverend looked round at the mention of the word traitor. 'Keep your voice down, Percy, lad. We don't know who might be eavesdropping.'

'Well, did you?' the curate repeated.

'Absolutely not,' Augustus Shackleford retorted, now using his best fire and brimstone voice. 'That was entirely the Froggy's idea.' He tucked his crossed fingers inside his cassock and stared at the curate innocently.

Percy narrowed his eyes. He'd spent so many years with the Reverend, he knew exactly when the old reprobate was pitching the gammon.

'I think...' the clergyman went on, only to pause as Finn came running up. 'Ah jus' seen one o' the sailors leavin' the ship,' he hissed, pointing to a shadowy figure walking down the gangplank.

'Tare an'hounds, the others aren't here yet,' the Reverend grumbled. 'If he's our traitor, ain't he supposed to wait until his absence is not likely to be noticed?'

'Ah dinnae think anyone explained that tae 'im,' Finn shrugged, 'an naeboddie be watchin' anyways. Shall ah gaun tell the Captain?'

'Has he told the crew about the change in destination?' Reverend Shackleford asked, watching the sailor's progress down the wharf.

'Ah dinnae kenn,' Finn answered, running along the deck to keep the man in sight.

'Thunder an' turf,' the Reverend grumbled. 'Why does every conspiracy we come across have to be so deuced complicated?' He shook his head in disgust as Finn began hopping up and down in nervous excitement, looking for all the world as though he was about to enter a boxing ring.

Augustus Shackleford ground his teeth in annoyance, unsure what to do. In the end, Finn made the decision for him. Shaking his head in frustration, the boy turned and ran towards the gangplank, Flossy at his heels.

'Fiend seize it,' Percy muttered in a rare display of temper. Then, by unspoken mutual consent, the two men lifted their cassocks and took off after the boy.

As they hurried along the wharf, the first carriage was arriving carrying Roan, Gabriel, Faith and Hope. Seeing the two clergymen heading towards them, Roan commanded the driver to stop and leaned out of the window.

'What's happened?' he demanded as the two clergymen came up alongside.

'I reckon our bloke's legged it,' Augustus Shackleford wheezed as Percy ran on ahead. 'Finn's on his tail.'

'Please don't do anything foolish, Father,' Faith called worriedly, leaning round her husband.

'Chance would be a fine thing,' the Reverend groaned, leaning against the side of the carriage. 'By the time I get there, it'll likely be all over bar the deuced shouting.'

'I think one of us should accompany you,' Gabriel announced, leaning forward to open the door.

Reverend Shackleford shook his head. 'Finn's headstrong, but the lad's not bird-witted. Just tell the Froggy.' And with that, he took off again.

'Damnation,' Hope muttered. 'Finn might not be bird-witted, but I can't say the same about Father.'

By the time Augustus Shackleford turned onto the main quayside, he could see no trace of either Percy or Finn. 'Thunder and turf,' he puffed, sitting down on a convenient lobster pot to get his breath back. A couple of minutes later, he caught sight of Percy coming towards him.

'Finn's vanished,' the curate reported, his face white.

The Reverend felt panic grip him the like of which he'd not felt since the incident with old Queen Charlotte and the duck-pond. 'He can't just have disappeared into thin air. Which way did he go?'

Percy shook his head, sitting down next to his superior. 'There are several small warehouses just before the end of the quay. I think he might have gone into one of 'em, but I daren't go in and look. If the lad's hiding, my arrival could give him away.' The curate looked as though he was about to cry, and for a second Augustus Shackleford felt like joining him.

'Did you see Flossy?' Percy shook his head. 'Well, in that case, it stands to sense they're both in hiding. It's what Finn and Flossy do best. If they'd been found, you'd have heard the deuced commotion from here.'

The Reverend laid his hands on his knees, thinking for a second. 'I think our best option is to get as close as we can to the warehouses without being seen,' he went on, his voice growing more decisive. 'The lad'll send Flossy for help if he needs it, so it's our job to be as close as possible, just in case.' He clambered to his feet. 'Come along, Percy, my man, there's no time to lose.'

Finn was undeniably proud of his ability to blend in with his surroundings whenever he needed to. It was a skill he'd learned as an orphan on the streets of Banalan, though he hadn't had cause to use it so much since Percy and Lizzie Noon had become his parents.

He slowed down as he got closer to his quarry, calling Flossy to him and strolling casually, while making sure to keep his distance. At the end of the main quay, the sailor turned to the left and was abruptly out of sight.

Picking Flossy up, he hurried towards the place he'd seen the deckhand disappear and peered cautiously round the corner. In front of him were three warehouses – or at least that's what they'd been in the beginning. Finn doubted they'd housed anything more than rats in a long time.

'What do you think, Floss?' he whispered. He cast his eyes slowly over the dilapidated buildings. Initially, he could see no sign of the man he'd been following until all of a sudden he spotted movement. A door opening and closing.

Finn felt his heart slam against his chest and wanted nothing more than to run in the opposite direction. But what good would that do? If he was going to discover anything useful, he had to get closer. Unfortunately, that meant crossing the very empty distance to the warehouses. After a moment's hesitation, he buried his head in Flossy's soft fur, gaining comfort from the little dog's warmth. Then, straightening his shoulders, he took a deep breath and stepped out into the open. Whistling softly, he sauntered across the empty piece of ground, looking for all the world as if he was enjoying a morning stroll.

With every step, he expected a sudden shout ordering him to stop, and by the time he reached the shadow of the first warehouse, he was trembling almost uncontrollably. Leaning against the sagging wall, he stayed put, allowing his quaking to subside while Flossy licked his ear.

Finally, after about five minutes, his shaking stopped, and he took a step away from the wall and crept towards the far warehouse where he could hear the sound of voices. All too soon, he reached the same door the sailor had vanished through, and tucking Flossy under his arm, he eased the door open. At the sudden sound of footsteps, the little dog started growling under her breath. Hushing her urgently, Finn tucked her small body inside his vest, freeing up both of his hands. 'We have to be quiet, Floss,' he murmured to the top of her head, 'but you need to be ready to run when I tell you.'

Carefully, he stepped into the gap made by the open door and peered into the gloom. He could just make out the back of the sailor standing at the other end of the room. He was facing another closed door, obviously waiting for something - or someone.

To Finn's right was a pile of old lobster pots, and as he heard the sudden echoing of footsteps, he quickly crouched behind them and peeped over the top. Seconds later, the door opened, and a man stepped through. To Finn's surprise, he looked like a toff. He was even wearing a top hat. The boy held his breath, straining to hear the conversation.

After a few seconds of mumbling, the deckhand raised his voice. 'I'm tellin' you, Sir, they're anchorin' at Solidor Bay outside St. Malo. The Captain told us, plain as day.'

'Did he say why?' For some reason, the cultured voice turned Finn cold. Helplessly, his stomach churned.

'I dunno, yer ludship, I ain't a Jack Tar by trade as yer know. Taffy's coverin' fer me.' There was a pause, and then the sailor spoke again, this time with more confidence.

'I know yer ludship wants this bloke in Davy Jones' Locker afore 'e gets to Montclair, an' I reckon I'm the man fer the job,' he declared. 'I'll slit 'is throat an' send 'im over the side wi out anyone 'seein' or 'earin' a thing.'

'You think you can do that?' The cultured voice sounded bored.

'No one'll even know 'e's gone,' came the boastful reply. Finn watched the toff stare down at the smaller man, his face expressionless in the gloom. He said nothing. Just... stared.

'But if a job's to be done right, it deserves a bit extra.' The sailor was babbling now, clearly reciting words he'd told himself over and over again. Finn watched, his heart suddenly in his mouth as the deckhand took a small step backwards.

'Is Taff onboard?' the man asked softly.

'Aye, yer ludship.'

'And he knows what must be done?' The sailor nodded.

'Have you told him your... little plan?' The sailor swallowed visibly and took another small step backwards. No stranger to violence, Finn gave a small moan and squeezed his eyes shut, instinctively knowing what was about to happen.

'You're quite right, sometimes a little extra is exactly what's required.' Finn heard a scuffle, then a muffled gasp, and when he opened his eyes, the sailor was sliding slowly towards the floor.

Holding his fist against his mouth in horror, the boy remained still, not daring to move a muscle. Seconds later, the toff gave a grunt and finally let the man drop. In his hand was a narrow, pointed blade. Leisurely bending down, he wiped it clean on the prone sailor's jacket. Then he slid it into a small sheath and slipped it inside his coat.

At that moment, the early morning sun came out from behind the clouds and shone directly through the window. It was too grimy to give much light, but there was just enough for Finn to notice a scar beginning at the base of the gentleman's thumb and disappearing up his sleeve. Unfortunately, before he could study it further, the sun disappeared, returning the room to shadow.

After one last look at the corpse lying at his feet, the man turned on his heel and quickly walked back the same way he'd arrived without a second glance.

For several seconds after the door slammed behind him, Finn remained where he was. That the sailor was dead, he had no doubt. The blood was slowly seeping out from a puncture wound in his side, pooling grotesquely on the floor.

Finn was no stranger to death, but the complete lack of concern exhibited by the stranger chilled him in a way he couldn't even begin to explain. But though he was terrified of moving, the boy knew he would be in far more danger if he stayed where he was. Toffs like *Mr Top Hat Man* didn't do their own dirty work, and he knew that somebody would be along soon to get rid of the body.

Slowly and carefully, he got to his feet, and keeping his eyes on the far door, backed quietly back towards the entrance he'd come through earlier.

As he finally slipped through the door, out into the blessed fresh air, Finn realised what it was about the killing that had made it extra horrifying. *Toffs didn't generally do their own dirty work.*

Mr Top Hat Man had killed the sailor himself because he enjoyed it...

Twelve

'Would you recognise him if you saw him again, lad?' Raphael's questioning was compassionate but matter of fact.

The combination worked, and Finn nodded, determinedly wiping away his tears with a grimy hand. 'Ah niver did see a muir terrible sight,' he declared with a shudder. 'That man – he enjoyed the killin'.'

They were seated in the Captain's cabin underneath the poop deck. The Reverend, Percy, Roan, Gabriel and Tristan were also present as Finn described what he'd seen.

'Do you think my son's in danger now?' Percy questioned the King's agent, his voice tight with worry.

Raphael shook his head. 'Whoever the killer was, he had no idea he was being observed.' He looked over at the boy, who was rapidly becoming much more himself. 'As awful as I know the experience must have been for you, Finn, your bravery has given us more than you can possibly imagine. We now know that there are or *were* two traitors onboard the ship and the one still living goes by the name of Taffy which is a nick-name given to men born in Wales. We also know that there is indeed someone directing things from the shadows. *Mr Top Hat Man*, as you very usefully called him, has made a grave error. But best of all – he doesn't realise it.'

The boy visibly swelled with pride and looked round with a wide grin, but before he had the chance to speak, Raphael continued, his voice turning stern.

'In truth, you were lucky today, Finn. It could easily have ended with you dead on the floor next to that sailor - and I doubt very much we'd have known your fate.' He held up his hand as Finn opened his mouth to protest. 'We will undoubtedly continue to need your help, young man. However, in the future, I must insist that you never lie, never act on impulse, and *never* do anything without first gaining the approval of your father.'

'Well, you can't argue with that, Finn, my boy,' the Reverend commented cheerfully. 'You've only got to look at me – following the rules has never done me any harm...'

~

The identity of their traitor hadn't been difficult to discover, since only one Welshman had been recruited in recent months. However, by the time everyone in their party had been informed, *Faith and Fortune* was under sail. Each person had been issued strict instructions to observe, nothing more, while Tristan was strongly advised to avoid going up on deck alone or giving any noticeable attention to his fiancée in the event it should be noticed.

Henrietta was especially confused. Though she couldn't be entirely certain, she was reasonably sure that Taffy wasn't the man she'd seen in the garden at Redstone House. Did that mean there might still be more than one traitor on board? Despite keeping a sharp lookout, she'd failed to spot him amongst the crew. She gnawed anxiously at her bottom lip. She hadn't mentioned the incident to her father, having assumed Raphael had done so. But then why had neither of them mentioned it?

After a few minutes, she sighed and determinedly put her concerns aside. There was undoubtedly a very good reason why it hadn't been brought up. Raphael had asked her to be vigilant, and she would continue to be so. If she caught sight of the man, she would inform the agent, but otherwise there were other, more urgent matters that required her attention – primarily tending to Roseanna, who'd unfortunately been struck down with the dreaded *mal de mer.* Percy too had been similarly afflicted and was being tended to by her mother and Aunt Hope.

Fortunately, by the time dinner was served in the Captain's private dining room, both patients had recovered sufficiently to be left alone.

'If the wind remains consistent, we should reach Perros-Guirec in under three days,' Roan stated after their plates had finally been taken away. He took a sip of his wine before lowering his voice. 'I understand that Lannion is roughly twenty miles inland, and Chateau Montclair is about three miles from the town. God willing, we'll reach it while Fontaine is still waiting at St. Malo. Hopefully, our traitor will try his luck tomorrow before we get close enough for him to swim to shore.'

'Hope is not quite the word I would use,' Tristan commented drily.

'My sympathies,' Rafe answered wryly, 'but if we can catch him in the act, we are more likely to get something useful out of him. He must realise that something untoward has happened to his shipmate by now, so with any luck he'll already be anxious and more likely to do something rash.'

'Again, I would argue there's nothing remotely *lucky* about either having one's throat cut or being thrown overboard,' Tristan disputed, 'even if one's murderer is excellent at improvisation.'

'Well, at least ye ken it be coming.' Dougal countered. 'Ah mean there must be a wee bit o' comfort in haein an idea o' the actual day someone be gaunnae kill ye. Mebbe we should toast tae that.' The Scot looked at his empty glass meaningfully.

Tristan thought for a moment before shaking his head. 'No, none,' he announced. 'In fact, I'll go further and state categorically that there is not one shred of comfort in knowing that tomorrow is the day I could well be departing this mortal coil.'

'The people you have around you will not allow you to depart anywhere,' Henrietta reassured him. 'Though if you do manage to get yourself murdered before the wedding ceremony, I've no doubt my cousin will kill you.'

'No one is being murdered tomorrow, or any other day,' Raphael avowed, looking at his fellow Frenchman. 'Though, once this is all over, I am expecting an invitation to the wedding.'

'If we succeed, you can be the bloody guest of honour,' Tristan quipped. Then, looking over at Dougal, he added, 'I think we can drink to that.'

Well aware she was probably being foolish, Henrietta nevertheless decided to take a stroll around the deck before retiring to her bed. Rosie had fallen into a fitful sleep after spending most of the day vomiting into a bucket, and Henri was loath to disturb her until she absolutely had to. It didn't help that the cabin had a foetid smell of sickness.

Putting on her warmest pelisse, Henrietta made her way to the foredeck. It was full dark, the sky completely clear and filled with so many stars it was though it was studded with diamonds. Shivering, she tucked her hands under her arms and made her way towards a small, makeshift seat she spied almost hidden under the foresail. Sitting down gingerly, she looked up at the heaving cloth propelling them along.

Her father had spent so much of his life aboard a ship, and she well knew that the ocean was as much a part of him as his own body. He might have left the Royal Navy, but he could no more have abandoned the sea than he could his own family. Her mother joked that the waves were his watery mistresses, but Henri knew Faith had long since come to accept that her husband would always have another life.

And sitting here staring up at the billowing sails, and the stars beyond, Henrietta thought she understood it. Until suddenly the stars were blotted out...

'May I join you, or would you prefer to be alone?' Raphael's deep voice brought her back to herself. Blinking, she looked up at the King's agent. To her surprise, she felt no sudden anxiety at his presence. It was as if he were as much a part of the fabric of *now* as she was. Somehow, they had both stepped out of the world – if only briefly.

She patted the space beside her and without saying anything further, he sat.

A comfortable silence reigned between them until at length, Henrietta glanced towards him and asked the question she'd been longing to pose since she first laid eyes on him.

'Why do you do it?'

Rafe looked down at his hands, resting against his knees. 'You want the truth?' he murmured without lifting his head.

'Yes.' Her voice was a whisper.

He did look at her then, his lips quirking in the enigmatic smile she'd seen him wear on so many occasions. Laughing at himself, she knew. She waited without speaking, and at first, she thought he wasn't going to answer.

And then...'I don't know.' His murmured response was the last thing she expected, and for a second, she was taken aback until he added, 'My father raised me to oppose the terror he believed had overtaken his country. From a boy, I understood what I was destined to do...' He paused, looked back down with a shrug. 'He never questioned whether it was what I wanted to do with my life, and neither did I. Until now.'

His last two words were almost inaudible, but Henrietta heard them, and after a moment, as though it was the most natural thing in the world, she slid closer. She could feel the welcoming, *familiar* warmth of his body as he wordlessly lifted his arm and pulled her to him and, without hesitation, she laid her head on his shoulder. They said nothing further about what had gone before. It was as though they were two souls adrift. No guarantees, no promises.

They simply sat and watched the horizon, empty except for stars filling the sky like a sparkling blanket. The murmurs of the crew on watch, and the ringing of the ship's bell every half hour faded until there was only the two of them. Finally, she felt him look down at her, his lips sliding against her hair, and she lifted her eyes to his. Slowly, unhurriedly, he bent his head until his lips were barely touching hers, then he waited – for her permission. Wordlessly, she lifted her arm and slid her hand around the nape of his neck.

It was all the encouragement he needed, and with a low groan, his lips finally took hers fully. Unlike the last time, the kiss was soft as he teased open her mouth, sliding his lips along hers, lingering, savouring the taste of her. Gradually, the kiss intensified, until she could feel him trembling with the effort of holding himself back.

This was his promise, his guarantee. If she wanted him, he was hers. Henrietta knew it with every fibre of her being.

When they finally parted, she slid her hand down to his shoulder and rested her forehead against his chest until abruptly the world came back as the ship's bell began ringing again. This time it finally stopped at eight as one of the ship's boys called out, 'Eight bells of the first watch, and all's well.' As a seafarer's daughter, Henrietta realised it must be midnight - the beginning of the middle watch - and pulled back with a sigh.

'Well, at least we can be thankful no one's gone overboard yet,' Raphael murmured drily. He pressed a kiss to her forehead as he rose to his feet. 'You should rest, Miss Carew. I doubt very much that things will remain as peaceful once the sun comes up. We will all need to be on our guard.'

Henrietta gave a sigh as she stood up. 'I really think under the circumstances you should call me by my given name,' she announced, straightening her skirt. 'At least when we're alone, anyway.'

Ignoring the noise from the change in watch, Raphael gave her a rueful smile. 'I doubt we will have another opportunity to hide away like this before we reach land, so I will bid you goodnight... *Henrietta*.' He gave a small bow before adding softly, 'Sleep well, chérie.' The endearment coupled with the intimate way he pronounced her name completely stole her breath as he turned abruptly and stepped through to the forward deck.

Heart pumping wildly, she watched as he paused to converse with one of the sailors who'd just come up on watch. Away from the darkness of the sails, the moon bathed the two men in an almost otherworldly light, and just as Henri was about to return to her cabin, the deckhand nodded at something Raphael said and turned towards her.

It was the man she'd seen sitting in the garden at Redstone House.

'Thunder an' turf, who forget to mention the simple deuced fact that we'd be sleeping in *hammocks*?' Reverend Shackleford's appalled whisper echoed throughout the lower deck, earning him a chorus of abuse from the sailors who'd just finished their watch.

'Oh, ah dinnae ken, ah reckon it be cosh,' Finn retorted, pulling off his boots. 'Ye cannae sleep on the floor, Revren.' Without further ado, the boy jumped onto the hammock and nimbly flipped onto his back, quickly joined by Flossy. Reverend Shackleford watched in horror. Every movement the boy had made could potentially see an old man like him on the floor with a broken leg or worse.

He looked over at the few proper beds situated around the edge of the deck. One of them was occupied by Percy, who looked as though he'd already done his time in Davy Jones' Locker. The only positive in the whole deuced bag of moonshine was that Dougal couldn't get into his bed either.

'But it's midnight,' the Reverend moaned. 'I'd have started getting ready for bed before dinner if I'd known. At this rate, it's going to take me the rest of the night to climb into the deuced thing.'

'Ah cannae argue wi' ye there,' Dougal declared, eyeing the hammock with the enthusiasm he'd normally reserve for Sassenachs and God botherers – in that order. 'Dae ye reckon there be a knack tae it?'

'Jus' hold the side's an' climb on,' Finn advised, pulling his blanket up to his chin to tuck Flossy in. 'But ye better goan wi' it, else ye'll be countin' yer toes come mornin'.'

'Dinnae fash yersel' Augustus, ah hae an idea,' the Scot announced suddenly. 'Hoo aboot ye hold ma hammock still, an' ah'll climb up. Then soon as ah be in it, ah'll hold yours still, an ye can dae the same.'

With an aggrieved sigh, the Reverend pushed his own hammock aside and took hold of Dougal's.

Naturally, by this time the sailors surrounding them had given up trying to sleep and were watching the proceedings with obvious enjoyment. There was even a spur-of-the-moment wager going on.

'Noo then...' the Scot declared, spitting on each hand and rubbing them on his breeches for luck.

'Gie it laldy,' Finn whispered enthusiastically, just as Dougal launched himself forward, yelling, 'Scoootland,' much in the same way as he'd always imagined his ancestors had done at Culloden. Unfortunately, his landing wasn't quite *Bonnie Prince Charlie*, and as he crashed sideways onto the hammock, it swung out wildly before somersaulting him straight onto the deck.

Instinctively, the Reverend ducked as the now empty hammock swung back towards him. 'Tare an' hounds, that was a close one,' he muttered, just as the rope holding the hammock began to unravel, dumping the entire bed directly on top of Dougal's prone form, eliciting a muffled groan from beneath the canvas, as well as an impromptu round of applause from the watching crew.

Thirteen

Fortunately, Rosie didn't wake as Henrietta climbed into the bed after escaping the foredeck without being spotted. Pulling the blanket up to her chin, Henri lay staring into the dark, her mind immediately revisiting her earlier misgivings. Naturally, the most significant was whether Raphael was already acquainted with the sailor - and if he was, how did they know one another?

Henrietta took a deep breath. She was entirely jumping to conclusions. Putting her feelings aside, Raphael Augustin had given no cause for her to think he might be playing both sides. A brief conversation with a member of the crew did not make him a traitor, and in truth, he'd shown no concern that she might be watching. Surely if he'd been involved in something illicit, he would have at least tried to do it out of her sight?

Gradually, she felt her heart rate begin to slow down. The next couple of days would be difficult enough without her fertile imagination making it worse.

Raphael had vowed to ensure Tristan reached Montclair alive and well to claim his inheritance.

She had to trust that the man she was rapidly falling in love with would deliver on his promise.

~

The next morning the wind had lessoned, though happily it hadn't changed direction. Roseanna and Percy were fortunately both feeling much better and had even managed to swallow some toast. Unfortunately, aside from that, breakfast was a dismal affair with everyone on edge. Indeed, Tristan was the only one remotely cheerful, which, given that he was the intended victim, simply made everyone else feel worse.

In the end, it was decided that Tristan would go up on deck every half an hour surrounded by a selected set of three people – one woman and two men. Naturally, they had to vary it to avoid giving the game away – though the Reverend argued that no man was so popular that everyone on the deuced ship wanted to spend time with him.

In the first *perambulation,* he would be directly accompanied by Roan, Gabriel and Faith. However, when Tristan reasoned that having both Roan and Gabe with him definitely looked suspicious, they substituted the Viscount for Dougal. Tristan's look of alarm was accompanied by a muttered comment that was unrepeatable in front of ladies...

The rest of them would be scattered around the ship, endeavouring to look as nonchalant as possible – though it didn't help that Percy's idea of nonchalance was to attach Finn to him with a rope, much to the boy's disgust.

Indeed, the whole thing was in grave danger of turning into a farce as Dougal loudly pronounced the deck free o' any shady characters after bravely declaring himself willing to be the *sacrificial anode* – a term he'd heard one of the sailors use the day before. While he wasn't entirely certain what an anode was exactly, he thought the phrase had a nice ring to it.

When nothing had happened by lunchtime, Raphael was tempted to throw Tristan overboard himself just to reduce the anxiety.

'I don't see why we can't just lock the varmint in the deuced hold and be done with it,' Reverend Shackleford grumbled, helping himself to some cheese and biscuits as they sat down for lunch. 'Why do we have to wait for him to try and shove Tristan overboard first?'

Raphael gritted his teeth. 'If we simply lock the blackguard up, we'll have nothing to bargain with, and we need to find out exactly what he knows.'

'Could there be another traitor onboard?' Henrietta asked, her voice carefully detached. 'I mean one we're not aware of?' She stared at Raphael as she spoke, willing him to say something, *anything* to set her mind at rest. She had spent the entire morning agonising over what she'd seen the night before. Despite her vow to trust Raphael, she'd been unable to rid herself of the image of him exchanging banter with the sailor. The easy casualness that indicated so clearly that the two knew each other.

But instead of offering any reassurance, the Frenchman remained silent - but more than that, he didn't even look at her. Henri felt a huge lump form in her throat, as her certainty of the night before abruptly dissolved.

Roan looked at his daughter with a frown. 'Well, since the crew numbers less than twenty-five in total, I think it unlikely. Do you have a particular reason for asking?'

Henrietta fought the urge to cry as everyone turned towards her.

'Is there something you're not telling us, Henri?' Roan asked, his tone short.

Henrietta turned to her father. 'I saw a man wearing *Fortune's* colours skulking in the garden at home...' She paused and looked back at Raphael before adding in a whisper, 'The same man I saw Mr Raphael Augustin speaking with last night on the foredeck.'

All eyes turned to the King's agent, the silence thunderous.

Raphael remained perfectly calm, though Henri wanted to cry at the regret she read in his eyes.

'The man in question works for me,' he said quietly. 'He has been aboard the *Faith and Fortune* since just after Blackmore.'

'You placed a man on *my* ship without informing me?' Roan's voice was low and furious.

Raphael stared back at him impassively. 'You admitted to having saved Tristan's life at the same time as rescuing a French insurrectionist from prison. In truth, I found your story hard to swallow and needed confirmation that it wasn't a complete Banbury story.' He hesitated and spread his hands. 'After Miss Carew overheard Fontaine's men speaking in the Poulton's Hotel, I thought it best to leave him in place.'

'Why didn't you tell me the truth once we suspected *Fortune* had a turncoat on board?' Roan shot back.

There was a short silence, then Raphael sighed. 'Because I didn't know what Jacob would find. What if the man secretly working for Fontaine turned out to be someone you've known for years? You are too close, Roan. You said it yourself, many of these men have been with you since they were boys.'

Roan gritted his teeth. He knew what the Frenchman stated was true.

'What was he doing in the gardens?' Henrietta asked suddenly, her voice hoarse.

'He was waiting for me,' Rafe responded calmly.

Henrietta eyed him narrowly, anger beginning to overtake the hurt. 'Well, clearly I wasn't *astute* enough to recognise that,' she retorted, her voice carrying a wealth of meaning meant for Raphael alone. Then, biting her lip, she looked down at her untouched food, but not before she saw something in the Frenchman's eyes. Something more than just regret. Lifting her napkin from her lap, she replaced it on the table and got to her feet. 'I think I shall leave you to your deliberations,' she said to her father. 'I have nothing more to add and would very much like some air.'

'Do you feel unwell, darling?' Faith asked, looking over at her daughter in concern.

Henrietta shook her head, desperate now to leave the claustrophobic cabin. 'I'm just not very hungry. I promise not to do anything foolish,' she added, sensing an impending warning before it was uttered.

'Would you like me to accompany you?' Roseanna asked, putting down her own napkin. Looking over at her cousin, seated next to Tristan, Henrietta felt her throat tighten. Despite all the fear and uncertainty, their happiness, their *closeness*, was unmistakable. She shook her head, knowing she needed to get out before she made a complete fool of herself.

'I'll come with you, lass.' Henri looked over at her grandfather in surprise as he pushed back his chair. 'You coming, Percy?' he added, looking over at his curate.

'An' me,' Finn interrupted, stuffing the rest of his cheese hurriedly into his mouth and putting another couple of lumps into his pocket for later.

'Well, dinnae jus' blether aboot it, gaun jus' bugger aff with ye,' Dougal chimed in irritably, waving his hand towards the door. Plainly the Scot's earlier notion of self-sacrifice had run its course, and he was back to simply relishing the conflict. 'Bloody Sassenachs,' he muttered, helping himself to another hunk of bread.

Knowing the futility of arguing with her grandfather, Henrietta simply nodded her head and all but bolted for the door, Finn already at her heels with Flossy tucked under his arm.

Regretfully, Percy put down his knife. While conflict at the dinner table generally gave him indigestion, it was difficult to turn his back on a nice, ripe Stilton.

'Get a move on, Percy,' Reverend Shackleford grumbled from the door. 'God only knows what mischief Finn is up to with nobody on the other end of his tether.' The last was said in jest, but it had the desired effect. Seconds later, the door closed behind them.

For a few seconds, no one spoke. The three women at the table, recognising Henrietta's distress, instinctively looked towards its cause.

Aware of their scrutiny, Raphael's lips tightened, but he refused to be drawn.

'Who the devil is this Jacob anyway?' Roan ground out. 'You gave us the impression that you were unable to trust anyone in your organisation.'

'He's not part of my organisation,' Raphael responded tightly. 'He works for me and has done so for over ten years – ever since I found him begging on the streets of London.'

'How strange,' Hope observed tartly, 'I feel like I've heard a similar tale very recently.'

Rafe bristled but managed to keep his temper in check, well aware that she was simply voicing what everyone else in the room was thinking. 'I was wrong to have kept it from you,' he bit out finally, 'but I...'

'No,' Roan shot back. 'You were wrong to have insinuated your man onto my ship in the first place. You want us to trust you, yet you do not reciprocate. You of all people should know that trust works both ways – especially when lives are at risk.'

The two men glared at each other, neither backing down.

'I do not play both sides,' Rafe bit out. 'But you are right, I have asked much of you – *all* of you - without giving anything in return...' He stopped, rubbing his brow in frustration before continuing in an equally intense, but much quieter tone, 'If we are to stand any chance of securing Tristan's inheritance and putting an end to Fontaine's plotting, we have no choice but to continue on this path. He and his associates are willing to commit cold-blooded murder simply to rid themselves of Montclair's rightful heir. They have already attempted to blow up two prominent members of the British Parliament with no care as to how many more would die in the blast. They nearly managed to assassinate the King, for God's sake. Whatever you think of me, we cannot falter now. You *know* we cannot.'

A stony silence met his words, but a second later, Roan took a deep breath and finally nodded. 'From now on, you hold nothing back,' he ordered sharply, unmindful that he wasn't speaking to a subordinate.

Gritting his teeth at the other man's highhanded tone, Rafe nevertheless gave a curt nod. He followed it with a quick, instinctive glance towards the door, before ruthlessly pushing aside the crushing regret at having lied to Henrietta.

The mission was all that mattered now.

Up on deck, Henri took a deep breath, welcoming the buffeting wind. Despite her efforts to push the agent out of her mind, she couldn't halt the picture in her head of Raphael staring down at her, eyes slumberous with need. Desperately, she tried to banish the image, but her mind refused to comply. Blinking back sudden tears, she made her way up to the poop deck and sat on one of the few benches provided for officers and passengers. Seconds later, she buried her face in her hands despairingly. She couldn't rid herself of the notion that *everything* he'd said to her had been a lie. That he couldn't be trusted.

'Be ye sad, mistress?' a small voice asked seconds later. Her eyes flew open, and she found herself looking into the thoughtful eyes of Finn Noon. The boy was staring at her worriedly, obviously unsure whether he needed to fetch another adult, or stay with her in case she threw herself overboard.

'I am perfectly well, Finn, thank you,' she murmured, wiping her eyes hurriedly and making a heroic effort to smile. 'It's just that everything is so…' she broke off, trying to find the right word.

'Skeerie,' the boy helpfully provided, sitting down beside her and placing Flossy in his lap. 'Dinnae fash yersel, Miss Henri, ye nae be th'only one. Honest tae God, ah niver in ma life been so afeart as ah be yesterday.'

'You were very brave,' Henrietta told him truthfully. Finn nodded matter-of-factly. 'Ma Da reckons ah be turnin' his hair grey, but ah dinnae think so since he dinnae hae any hair.' The boy chuckled, and looking at his cheerful face, Henri found herself smiling back.

Seconds later, the Reverend and Percy arrived, heralded by a soft bark from Flossy. 'Tare an' hounds, it's blowing a deuced gale up here,' Augustus Shackleford complained, climbing the stairs towards them. Finn obligingly shifted on the bench and patted the space he'd created.

'I hope you've not been bothering Miss Carew,' Percy quizzed him.

'Nae, Da, me an' Miss. Henri hae bin enjoyin' a wee banter. She be desperate sad, though ah dinnae ken why.'

Percy winced as he sat down. 'Please forgive my son's forthrightness, Miss Carew,' he implored. 'The lad means well but doesn't grasp that it's not always acceptable to say whatever is in his head.'

'That's why the boy's always in the deuced basket,' Reverend Shackleford chuckled, sitting down and tucking his hands under his cassock. 'If it's the Frog who's upset you, lass, I suggest you put him out of your mind immediately. Slippery, that one.'

Henrietta looked at the earnest faces of her companions and shook her head. 'Nobody has upset me, Grandfather,' she hedged. 'I'm simply anxious over what is to come.'

'You youngens are far too sensitive nowadays,' the Reverend went on, shaking his head. 'In days gone by, me and Percy would've laughed in the face of danger – ain't that right, Percy lad?'

The curate nodded dutifully, though his expression told a different story. Unexpectedly, Henri stifled a giggle. She opened her mouth to speak, when Finn suddenly jumped off the bench and hurried to the taffrail surrounding the poop deck, leaning forward to peer over the main deck. Seconds later, he turned back. 'Ah jus' seen that sailor gaun doon tae the lower deck.'

The Reverend frowned. 'You're sure it was him?'

'Aye,' Finn nodded vigorously. 'Ye reckon he be up tae nae good?'

'Well, I doubt he's going for a nap,' Augustus Shackleford frowned. He turned to his curate. 'Come on, Percy, this is our chance to nobble the blackguard.'

'I'm not sure that's a good...' started Percy, only to realise the Reverend was already hurrying down to the main deck. With a sigh, he got to his feet. 'Stay here, Finn, he ordered the boy,' before reluctantly following his superior down the companionway.

Hopping from one foot to another, Finn waited until the two men had vanished down the ladder, before running back to Henrietta. 'Ah cannae stay here like a feartie, Miss Henri. Dae ye look after Flossy.' With that, he plonked the little dog into Henrietta's arms and hurried after the two men.

'Wai...' Henri began, but the boy was already on the main deck. Getting to her feet, she hastened to the taffrail and watched the boy start down the ladder leading to the lower deck. 'Damn,' she muttered to herself. Should she go and inform Raphael and her father? They'd still be at the table having lunch. Biting her lip, she hesitated, loath to go back into the dining room just yet. But at the end of the day, she had no choice. She couldn't leave her grandfather and Percy to run headlong into possible danger – not to mention Finn. She looked down at the little dog in her arms, who was whining softly. 'I know, Flossy,' she muttered, 'bacon-brained, the bloody lot of them.' Then with a sigh, she headed down towards their private quarters to speak with the one person she'd hoped to avoid.

Fourteen

‘I think the varmint’s going down into the hold,’ whispered the Reverend as Percy tiptoed up behind him. Hidden behind a large barrel, they watched the sailor rummage around in the gloom.

‘What’s he looking for?’ the clergyman muttered.

‘We should go and tell Mr Augustin,’ Percy suggested in an urgent undertone.

‘And what good would that do now? The Lord knows what mischief the scoundrel could be up to in the time it takes us to get back up top. He could well blow up the deuced ship.’

‘Aye, ah cannae imagine the bampot be gaun fer a jobbie.’ The small voice came from directly behind them, causing both men to jump and swing round in sudden panic.

‘What the devil do you think you’re doing, Finn?’ the Reverend quizzed in a furious whisper. ‘You nearly gave me a deuced apoplexy.’

Percy groaned. ‘I told you to stay with Miss Carew.’

‘Ah cannae dae that, Da. Ye might need ma help.’

The curate was about to argue when a sudden noise had all three of them turning back towards their quarry, just in time to see him pull out a large knife from underneath a stack of what looked like old sailcloths.

'Thunder an' turf,' Reverend Shackleford muttered, 'what the deuce is he going to do with that?'

'Be he gaunnae cut off somebody's head?' Finn asked, his voice a mixture of fear and ghoulish excitement.

'Shut up, Finn.' The heated whispers came back in unison.

As they watched, the sailor stepped towards the ladder leading down into the hold. 'I was right,' the Reverend crowed. 'But he'll need more than a deuced knife to blow up the ship. What's the varmint up to? Come on.'

Percy gave a small moan as he tiptoed after the Reverend. 'You stay here, Finn,' he whispered, though his tone clearly indicated he thought there was more chance of hell freezing over.

As they reached the ladder leading down into the hold, the Reverend got down on his hands and knees, then, grabbing hold of Percy's cassock to stop him falling headfirst into the gaping hole, he slid onto his stomach.

'What on earth are you doing, Sir?' the curate asked in a panicked whisper.

'I'm going to have a quick look at what the blackguard's up to. Get ready Percy, we might need to move quickly.' The curate looked down disbelievingly, thinking it might actually take them the rest of the trip to get the Reverend up off the floor. Even worse, the goosecap was now inching forward to hang his head down through the hole.

Hurriedly, the curate knelt down and took hold of the Reverend's legs, indicating Finn should sit on his ample bottom.

'Ouch, careful,' Augustus Shackleford whispered heatedly, 'I don't want to end up with splinters in me nutmegs.'

As he slowly inched forward, Percy's feeling of dread increased. 'Can you see anything yet?' he hissed as the Reverend's chest slid down level with the ladder.

There was a brief silence, followed by a strangled sound. 'Tare an' hounds, the deuced varmint's trying to cut the tiller ropes,' came the hoarse whisper. 'We've got to stop him else none of us will make it to France.'

'What can we do, Sir?' Percy uttered a small moan as the Reverend slid down further until Finn's feet were dangling in midair over the edge of the hole.

'I can't hold you much longer,' Percy groaned. 'You need to come back up, Sir... Finn, what the devil are you doing?'

The boy's feet had found purchase on the first rung of the ladder, allowing him to stand. 'You pull the Revren' back up, Da,' he whispered excitedly, 'an' ah'll goan gie that bampot a skelpit lug he'll niver forget.'

'No, lad, it's too dangerous,' Percy hissed just as Finn accidentally trod on the Reverend's fingers, which were gripping the first rung as though his life depended on it – which it probably did. A stifled moan drifted up.

'Sorry, Revren,' the boy muttered, trying to find the next rung down with his other foot and inadvertently kicking the clergyman's ear in the process.

In the meantime, the sawing sound continued apace.

In desperation, Percy threw himself on top of his superior, clutching the flailing legs as they both slid inexorably towards the opening, inch by agonising inch.

Just when it looked as though all three of them were going to become intimately acquainted with the deck below, a small whirlwind of fur appeared at the top of the hole and gave a short bark.

Hearing the noise, Taffy looked back and nearly jumped out of his skin as he caught sight of what looked like a giant bat hanging upside down on the ladder.

'Stop, you craven, lily-livered blackguard,' shouted the Reverend, realising the time for secrecy was well and truly past.

In answer, the sailor turned back to his task with renewed urgency.

By now, they could hear feet pounding down the lower deck ladder behind them, but help had come too late to stop the catastrophe.

Looking up at the little dog's eager face, Finn pointed down to the desperate deckhand and yelled, 'Stop him, Floss.'

She needed no further urging. Using the Reverend as a makeshift slide, Flossy was at the bottom of the ladder in seconds. Without hesitation, she made for the traitor's ankle, causing him to fall back with a cry. As the dog's teeth closed around his foot, he tried to roll over, brandishing the knife and kicking out in an effort to dislodge her.

But this was Flossy's speciality. Nimbly she danced round the sailor's jabbing hands and feet, growling and barking, while behind her, the Reverend was yanked unceremoniously back up through the hole.

Seconds later, Roan slid expertly down the ladder, closely followed by Raphael, Tristan and Gabriel. Without hesitation, Roan kicked the knife out of the traitor's hand and felled him with a single punch before turning to the damaged tiller rope.

'It won't last much longer,' he rasped. 'You'll need to give me a hand to hold it together. Finn, go up top and shout for help. Tell them it's the tiller rope.'

'For God's sake, man, what in blazes were you thinking? Sabotaging the tiller ropes would have seen us all in Davy Jones' Locker – you included.' Roan stared at the sailor in frustration.

Tied to a chair in the Captain's cabin, the traitor was terrified but defiant, and his only response was a careless shrug.

'You must have received a considerable sum to take such a risk,' Raphael observed calmly. 'Who paid you?' Sullen silence was his answer, and Rafe shook his head and smiled.

It was nothing like the smile Henrietta had been favoured with - this was a promise from someone who was well versed in getting information out of unwilling informants. 'If you don't help us, the best you can hope for is the rope,' Raphael continued conversationally. 'You know that. Did you believe that once we lost control of the ship, you'd be close enough to France to swim ashore? If so, I think you miscalculated. We are still a day out from our destination.'

The sailor glared up at the agent, but sweat was forming on his brow as his defiance began to fracture.

'Do you think I care what state you are in when I deliver you to the authorities?' Rafe questioned him. He gestured towards his companions, standing in uncomfortable silence. 'These men might be honourable, but my job leaves no room for chivalry. Make no mistake, I will do *whatever it takes* to extract the information we need.'

'Can't be any worse than what the bloody toff'll do to me if I rat 'im out,' Taffy spat in one last show of bravado.

'Can it not?' Rafe responded softly.

Seconds later, the man crumbled. 'Called himself Mr Smith, but I knew that weren't 'is name. 'Ow many bloody *Smiths* are there with wearing a fancy ring – an' over a pair o' gloves.'

'Did you recognise anything unusual about it?' Rafe interrupted sharply.

'Na, I only got a quick glimpse.' He shrugged. 'Just noticed he had the ring over the top of 'is gloves – I mean who does that for Christ's sake. More like a bloody macaroni than a nob.'

'Where did you meet him?'

'Tavern in Plymouth. Asked if wos lookin' fer work. I told 'im I wos a Jack Tar, an' weren't lookin' fer a land job.

'So, 'e told me to get meself to Torquay to meet wi' someone called *Funtin*. Bloody Frog, jus' like the two o' you buggers...' He gave a snigger, showing a mouthful of rotten teeth. When Raphael simply stared at him impassively, his brief bravado fizzled out. 'There wos two of us. We wos both told to report to the *Fortune* an' wait fer orders.' He slumped back into his chair, the last of his swagger gone. 'I din't know about the *accident* they wanted 'im to 'ave,' he muttered, nodding his head towards Tristan, 'until I 'ad a message from 'is ludship tellin' me Jim weren't comin' back to the ship an' it were up to me to do the deed.'

'Did you know Jim was dead?'

Taffy nodded. 'Aye. Sent me a bit o' the bastard's ear wi' the note.' He gave a sigh. 'I'm no bloody murderer to off somebody in cold blood. The tiller ropes wos the best I could do.'

'So you'd kill everybody onboard rather than just one?' Roan cut in incredulously.

The sailor shrugged. 'Din't seem quite so *personal*.'

For a few moments nobody spoke, then Rafe turned a chair around in front of the captive and sat down, resting his arms on the back.

'I want you to listen and think on what I say,' the Frenchman commented levelly. The sailor frowned but nodded.

'There's only one way you'll avoid the rope – and that's if you cooperate.'

Taffy stared back at him warily, waiting.

'Tell Fontaine you've done as you were asked. That Tristan de Montclair is no more...'

'And?' The sailor clearly knew there was more to come.

Rafe leaned forward. 'Get me a name...'

'Wot if I decide to tell Funtin everythin'?'

'Then your days will be numbered in single figures. You know it, and I know it. But if you help us, I swear you will walk free when this is over.'

Henrietta paced the deck wondering what was being said inside her father's cabin. 'If yer tryin' tae get a wee spot o' exercise, lass,' Dougal muttered, 'could ye dae it elsewhere? Ah be fair puggled watchin' ye.'

'What does puggled mean?' Henri asked, stopping to look at the Scot.

'Weary, lass. An' right now ma bones be feelin every step.'

'As much as I hate agreeing with Dougal on principle,' her grandfather muttered, 'you might want to save your energy for when we anchor in Perros-Guirec tomorrow. That's when the real smoky business will start.'

'I cannae wait,' Finn enthused. 'Will there be lots o' fightin wi real swords an' stuff?'

'There won't be anything like that,' Percy scoffed. Monsieur Augustin will simply announce to the world that Tristan is the heir, and that will be that.

The other four, including Finn, looked at the curate with varying degrees of disbelief.

'That sailor tried to kill the lot of us, Percy lad. I reckon that's a good indication that the whole havey cavey business will be a bit more than a smile and a handshake.'

They'd taken refuge on the poop deck, watching the sun dip below the horizon. While Henrietta knew she'd have been welcomed in the Captain's cabin with her mother, aunt and cousin, somehow, after the events of the day, she felt a little detached from her female relatives. She knew they would ask questions about her assertion at lunch, and she simply couldn't face her mother's shrewd gaze when she skirted around the issue.

And anyway, dinner would be in another hour – if they'd finished questioning their traitor by then.

Henrietta wondered what would happen to him. The thought that he might take the morning drop filled her with horror – even though his actions could have killed them all.

'The Frog said he was gaun tae look fer somebody who might o' bin there when Tristan was a bairn,' Dougal declared thoughtfully. 'Mebbe whoever it were that took the lad tae… where it be?'

'Pontorson,' Henri supplied.

'Deuced needle in a haystack if you ask me,' Reverend Shackleford retorted. 'Whoever it was is most likely pushing up daisies by now.'

'There's bound to be someone who recognises Tristan,' Henrietta argued. 'I mean, he really is the image of his father. If enough people believe him the heir, then Claude Fontaine won't have a leg to stand on.'

'Ah doot it'll be that simple, lass,' Dougal bemoaned. 'Right now, we dinnae ken where the bastard is – is he waiting fer us in Montclair, or did he take the bait?'

'How far away is St. Malo?' Henrietta asked, finally sitting down on the bench.

Her grandfather shrugged. 'Far enough for us to reach Montclair before he does.'

'But what if he's waiting for us in the village?' Percy interrupted. 'We could be walking into a trap.'

'Ah cannae argue wi' ye, Percy,' Dougal sighed. 'But ah ken one thing. Them Frogs hae only ever fought wi' Sassenachs. They cannae begin tae ken what it be like tae face a true Scotsman wi a battle lust.'

'What be battle lust?' asked Finn with interest.

The Reverend chuckled. 'Whatever it is, I doubt Dougal's ever felt it.'

'Ah'll hae ye ken ma ancestors were at Culloden,' Dougal protested with a sniff. 'Ah dinnae need tae hae bin in a battle tae know what it feels like. It be in ma body.'

'What, like nits?' Finn questioned.

~

Dinner that night was a subdued affair. Taffy had been placed in Raphael's cabin under guard, and although the details his confession were shared with the rest of them, no one felt like celebrating – especially when Raphael coolly requested that his man remain undercover, even though their traitor had been caught.

Henrietta spent the whole meal fighting the urge not to cry. She was the only other person who knew the informant's identity, but Raphael had not looked her way until the very end, when he'd quietly, dispassionately, asked for her discretion. At her brief nod, he'd looked around the table. The inference was clear - the mission was far from over.

Fifteen

They reached Perros-Guirec just after dawn. Taffy was the first to leave the ship - rowed to the quayside after which he was to make his way to St. Malo and hopefully meet up with Fontaine and his men. The note that came with his less fortunate shipmate's ear told him that someone would be waiting for him at the Grand' Porte in St. Malo.

The plan was for the sailor to break both the good and bad news. The good news being that Tristan de Montclair had found a watery grave, and the bad – that the *Faith and Fortune* was not headed to Rotheneuf, as they'd been led to believe, but directly to Perros-Guirec and on to Lannion.

The fact that Tristan had supposedly been removed from the playing field had not simply ended the matter. Taffy had been instructed to tell Fontaine that they were intending to announce the would-be Marquis's fate to as many people as possible. The doubt cast upon Claude Fontaine would be damaging at the very least, and the adverse publicity certainly not to the liking of his shadowy master.

Rafe was counting on the fact that Fontaine would hasten back to Montclair, hoping to quash the damaging rumours before they had the chance to take hold.

Where they'd be waiting.

Raphael had no idea whether Taffy would be able to convince Fontaine of his nephew's death, but at the very least it would sow confusion and buy them more time. And as for the sailor discovering the name of Mr Top Hat Man... In truth, Rafe didn't hold out much hope. Claude Fontaine was undoubtedly the link, and he was unlikely to share what he knew unless forced. And despite his hard-nosed approach to the sailor's questioning, Raphael was not actually in the habit of torturing people. Unless it was absolutely necessary, of course.

In all honesty, they'd gained more intelligence than Rafe had actually expected. It might take time, but he was convinced they'd eventually find the mastermind behind the *Revisionists* and bring the bastard down.

Unfortunately, the elation he was accustomed to feeling at the thought of putting an end to such treachery was missing.

All he could see was Henrietta's disillusioned face.

~

It was decided that the crew would remain on board under the command of Spalding. Under no circumstances were they to go ashore in the event they were needed in Lannion. While only a few of the men had served during the war with Napoleon, the majority were proficient in the use of both musket and sword. The country might no longer be at war, the seas were swarming with opportunist pirates.

In the meantime, their party would initially head to an inn in the village close to the Montclair estate. If Tristan was to be recognised, it would be by people who'd spent their lives in service to the old Marquis.

By Raphael's estimation, they had three days at most before Fontaine and his men arrived. Ideally, the rumour of Tristan's identity and homecoming would have already spread beyond the local community by that time. More than that though, it was imperative Tristan be already installed in the Chateau by the time the supposed caretaker returned and declared him a pretender. At the end of the day, possession was nine-tenths of the law, and it would be much more difficult for Fontaine to refute his nephew's claim when said nephew was already ensconced within the Montclair estate.

It was early afternoon by the time they'd had themselves and all their luggage brought ashore, then another hour before they were able to summon sufficient carriages to take all of them to Lannion. Indeed, they attracted quite a bit of attention as they travelled in stately procession along the rutted road, but as Raphael had commented – every little helped. Hopefully, by the time they reached the inn outside the village of Montclair, their presence would have attracted plenty of attention.

Rafe himself had gone ahead to do an initial reconnaissance and set the scene for the party's arrival. While waiting, he seated himself in the bar, making sure to take a table that was in full view of the patrons coming and going.

At first, after ordering himself a glass of red wine, he was roundly ignored, then gradually the sideways glances became stares until finally, he was addressed directly by a jovial middle-aged man who's red, thread veined features indicated a life spent mostly outdoors.

As he'd expected, the questions were initially quite formal and stilted, but Rafe couldn't help noticing that nearly everyone present was unashamedly listening.

Naturally, the first two questions were his name and where he'd come from. He responded genially with his real name but added that he was an *avocat* with a practice in St. Malo.

'What's a fancy *avocat* doing in Lannion?' his inquisitor asked.

Rafe waited slightly before answering, and when he did, he took care to ensure his voice contained the right amount of gravity. and. 'I'm here with my client and his wife's family,' Rafe explained carefully. 'He was sadly raised an orphan but has reason to believe his birth parents came from this area.'

Naturally such an admission broke the ice entirely and Rafe listened carefully as speculations and suggestions came thick and fast.

Finally, he deliberately set the cat among the pigeons by asking about Chateau Montclair…

All he needed to do now was wait for Tristan's arrival. He suppressed an inward chuckle. Nobody in the bar had left, though likely many of them had things they needed to do. By his estimation, the rest of the party should be arriving within the hour. And then things would really get interesting…

~

As they waited for the carriages to arrive, Faith couldn't help but notice Henrietta's distant expression, so unlike her usual happy, no-nonsense self.

On witnessing her daughter's acerbic comments to Raphael Augustin the day before, she'd felt a sudden prickling of anxiety. Was there something between the Frenchman and Henrietta that she wasn't privy to?

The fact that Henri had left the table shortly afterwards suggested so. Unfortunately, in the hours since, Faith had found no opportunity to speak with her daughter alone – indeed, they'd hardly been in the same room together. Henrietta had for the most part been in the company of her grandfather, which was strange in itself, and gradually Faith realised that Henri was deliberately keeping her distance to avoid the discussion she knew her mother was waiting for.

Initially, Faith felt a stirring of frustration, followed by bewilderment. She and Henrietta had always been close, sharing most things in the way of friends rather than mother and daughter. With no title to worry about, manners and etiquette had not played such a large part in Henri's upbringing, and she'd always been encouraged to speak her mind and share her views.

But naturally such freedom did not include what Faith very much feared amounted to a reckless romantic entanglement with a French spy...

~

'Now don't get me wrong, young lady, as a general rule, I enjoy your company, but I can't help asking myself why exactly you're sitting in a carriage with three old toasts and one whippersnapper when you could be exchanging the latest gossip with the ladies in the next carriage.' The Reverend raised his eyebrows as he regarded his granddaughter with the same expression he usually reserved for Flossy when the little dog indulged in the incomprehensible habit of rolling in fox poo.

'Mebbe they be boring,' Finn suggested.

'Never say a lady's boring,' Reverend Shackleford recommended with a wince that suggested being on the end of a curtain lecture was quite possibly any man's worst nightmare.

'My Elspeth didnae hae a dour bone in her body,' Dougal announced suddenly, much to everyone's astonishment. 'A terrible hairy chin, mind, but full o' sunshine.' He nodded to himself, oblivious of his bemused audience before sighing and adding, 'Ah loved her, true, but ah cannae deny she haed a face like a skelped arse.'

'Did she hae a beard?' Finn quizzed him delightedly. 'Ah once saw a lady wi' a beard doon tae here.' He pointed at his knees, drawing Percy's frowning attention to the fact that they were the colour of Blackmore's cesspit.

'I don't think it' polite to discuss the lady's physical attributes,' Henrietta interrupted hastily. 'After all, the lady is not here to defend herself.'

Dougal grinned. 'Och, she niver had any trouble defending herself, lass. Ah once saw her knock a grown man on his arse fer gaein her a wink.'

'What did he do?' Percy asked, interested despite himself.

The Scot creased his brow in thought. 'Ah cannae remember, tae be honest. Ah reckon when he came roond a couple o' days later, he begged her tae forgie him. An' ah cannae say ah blame him seein' as his eye was as black as the Earl o' hell's waistcoat.'

There was a short silence punctuated by Flossy's snoring, then, with a sceptical *hmph*, the Reverend turned back to his granddaughter. 'Right then, Henrietta Carew, I'll say my piece and that'll be the end of it - though I do think this is a conversation you should be having with your mother.' Henri stared at him in alarm as he went on, 'I think we all know that your attack of the mulligrubs is due to the Frog, but if you think sulking will solve your problem, think again, girl. All it'll do is set up his bristles and if you're determined to set your cap at the fella – though in truth I've never heard anything so totty headed in my entire life – the only thing you can do is *talk* to him.'

Henrietta bit her lip. Her grandfather was right. She was behaving like a spoilt child. There was far too much at stake for Raphael to spend time pandering to a foolish girl. With a sniff, she confessed what had happened – not the kissing bit, naturally, but the fact that he'd lied to her.

'So, you think he should have risked the whole deuced mission to tell you what was going on...'

'No... I... that's not what I...' Henrietta began before stopping and throwing her hands in the air. 'Shouldn't any relationship worth having be based on mutual trust?' She blurted. 'That's what I heard Papa say when I left the dining room.'

'Yes, well, I reckon your father was staring up his own nether regions when he made that statement. If there's one thing I've learned, lass, it's that nothing is ever black and white. You ask Percy. He's spent most of his life making deuced bad decisions that have turned out to be good ones in the end.'

'Well, I'm not quite sure that's entirely true,' grumped the curate. 'One could argue that most of my bad decisions have actually been made by you, Sir...'

At the sound of carriages arriving in the inn's front courtyard, Rafe felt the first flickering of anxiety. What if Tristan wasn't recognised? There were some people in the bar that were old enough to remember the fate of the Marquis and Marquese, but most had only heard the story secondhand.

The one thing that gave the agent hope was the careful way in which those in the bar spoke about Montclair's caretaker. In his experience, such reluctance to say anything remotely damning meant one thing – fear.

And if they feared him, they would welcome the new Marquis – if not with open arms, then at least without opposition. All he needed was for enough people to see the uncanny resemblance to his father, then hopefully the floodgates would open.

'Is Monsieur Fontaine up at the Chateau now?' Rafe asked casually.

'He left last evening,' commented the innkeeper. 'Took quite a few of his men too - I heard them galloping past just before midnight.'

Raphael felt a surge of triumph. The bastard had taken the bait.

Seconds later he heard the unmistakable sound of carriages outside. Remaining in his seat, he took a sip of his wine and watched.

First in were Roan and Gabriel, both looking, he suspected, as anxious as he did. 'We're looking for rooms,' he announced to the innkeeper in passable French.

'You're English?' Rafe felt a tightening as the sea captain nodded, adding, 'Most of us anyway. Is that a problem, Monsieur?'

The innkeeper shook his head. 'Not to me. How many rooms are you looking for?'

'How many do you have?' Gabriel asked drily as Faith, Hope and Roseanna came through the door.

The innkeeper scratched his head. 'Five in total and nobody in them at the moment.'

'Then we'll take all five,' Roan responded as Henrietta came through the door behind the Reverend and Percy, closely followed by Dougal and Finn. The innkeeper frowned.

'How many of you are there?' he growled, raising his eyebrows.

'Just one more,' Roan answered, shrugging off his greatcoat with a cordial smile. Seconds later, Tristan walked in. With his pale face and set jaw, he looked for all the world as though he was ready for a fight. For a moment the buzz of conversation continued, then slowly, one by one, it died, as the patrons looked towards the man standing in the doorway.

A man who was the spitting image of the old Marquis de Montclair.

For a moment there was silence, then all of a sudden, a chair crashed to the floor as an elderly man sitting alone in the corner rose stiffly to his feet. 'My Lord Marquis?' he whispered, his voice wavering. 'Lord Philippe, is that you?'

Tristan turned towards the bent figure, now peering at him through rheumy eyes as though he was some kind of apparition. After a second, he pulled off his gloves, smiled and inclined his head.

'My name is Tristan,' he clarified. 'Philippe de Montclair was my father.'

Sixteen

January 16th 1806

Looking over at her sleeping son, Catherine de Montclair stilled her rocking and closed the book she'd been reading aloud. With a tender smile, she climbed to her feet, and after laying the book on the small table next to the child's bed, she bent down to place a soft kiss on his brow and tuck his blankets around him. The thick brocade curtains at the window and the fire leaping in the nursery grate ensured the room was warm and cosy, despite the recent snowfall. Such warmth wouldn't last for long if the fire was allowed to go out completely.

'I'm leaving now, Brigitte – please do not get up. Just remember to stoke up the fire and blow out the candles before you get into bed.'

The nursemaid looked up from her chair in front of the fireplace, where she was darning yet another pair of Tristan's breeches. 'Bien sûr, Madame la Marquise. I will turn in as soon as I have finished with this pair.' She smiled and shook her head. 'Truly, madame, I have no idea how he gets through so many pairs of breeches – he never even has the chance to grow out of them.'

Catherine chuckled as she made her way to the door. 'His current obsession with pirates is not helping.'

'At least he didn't manage to skewer the footman bringing his dinner,' Bridgitte commented with a grin.

Her mistress winced and sighed. 'Fortunately, Maurice is used to Tris hiding behind the door, but to be on the safe side, I think we'll need to ensure only wooden cutlery in the nursery. I'll speak with Madame Durand. Bonne nuit, Brigitte.'

'Bonne nuit, madame.'

As the Marquise made her way downstairs, she glanced outside. The snow was falling steadily, but for some reason the flakes were flickering with light. Frowning, she stepped closer to the window and looked out over the courtyard to the twisting road beyond. It took her eyes a few seconds to adjust, and initially she wasn't entirely sure what she was seeing, but after another moment she recognised what the flickering lights actually were.

Torches – being carried by at least two dozen men. In their other hands, they held muskets.

Struggling to understand, Catherine stood rooted to the spot, until abruptly her paralysis was broken by a shout. '*Ferme la porte* – close the gate. We are under attack.'

With a low moan, Catherine picked up her skirts and hurried down the stairs, where she was met by her husband. 'What's happening, Philippe?' she gasped, gripping his arms. 'Who are those men?'

The Marquis shook his head. 'I have no idea. We need to wait and see what they want.

'If it were anything good, they wouldn't be carrying arms,' Catherine insisted. 'Do you think Claude is with them?'

Philippe took her in his arms. 'I cannot believe my brother would return bearing arms,' he insisted.

Catherine pulled away, her frustration vying with desperation. 'He wants what you have, Philippe. We both know that. And he hates that he can't have it.'

'Perhaps I can talk to him,' Philippe declared, his voice agonised. 'He might listen to me even now.

'My love, *listen* to yourself. You say what you want to believe. But in your heart, you know Claude will never be satisfied with your charity. He wants everything you have. *Everything*.

'When you discovered his treachery, you knew in your heart he'd return. We both knew it.' Her husband closed his eyes, despair washing over him, just as the pounding started on the gate.

Determinedly forcing her fear deep down inside, Catherine gave a small sob. 'We cannot let him have Tristan,' she whispered. 'Whatever happens tonight, our son is Montclair's future...' She paused and dashed at her eyes as she heard the gates begin to splinter.

Resting his head against hers, Philippe de Montclair abandoned the pretence that his half-brother meant them no harm. No matter what he'd done, or how hard he'd tried, the Marquis had never been able change the one thing that had eaten away at Claude from the day he'd discovered the name of his real father.

Claude Fontaine was a bastard – and always would be. Nothing could change that. All the love in the world couldn't change that.

Philippe had wanted to elevate him. To give him a formal place in his household. But it wasn't enough. Claude didn't want to be like Philippe. He wanted to *be* Philippe.

The final straw had been Tristan's birth. Something inside his half-brother had broken when he'd stared at the heir in his crib, and subconsciously, Philippe began to fear for his son's life. Until one day his brother simply disappeared. Despite extensive searches, Claude had seemingly vanished into thin air, and with the Peninsular War raging in both France and Spain, Philippe was finally forced to stop looking.

But in his heart of hearts, the Marquis always suspected that he hadn't seen the last of his brother and recent revelations had changed what had always been hope to fear. Catherine was right, the only person Claude cared about was himself.

Gripping his wife's shoulders, he looked deeply into her tear-filled eyes. 'You must take Tristan and leave now, ma chère. Go to the house in Pontorson and wait there until you hear from me.'

By the time he'd finished, his wife was already shaking her head. 'I won't leave you Philippe – and even if I did, Claude would only come after me. If we want Tristan to survive, we must put our trust in others.'

Philippe gritted his teeth, fighting back tears of his own.

'Tell Brigitte to get the boy dressed. I will find Antoine. The three of them can escape through the tunnels.

'But we have to be quick. The gates will not hold for much longer, and once they are in the courtyard, there are only the front doors between us and them. Bring Tris and Brigitte to the library. Antoine will meet you there.'

Minutes later, Catherine was feverishly dressing her son while his nursemaid grabbed what she could. Tristan at five years old stood wide-eyed in the candlelight and didn't object as they bundled him up and rushed back down the stairs.

Minutes later, she and Philippe gave their precious boy one last fierce hug, pressed a bag of coins into Antoine's hands and watched as Tristan was taken into the underground tunnels that were almost as old as Montclair itself.

Seconds later, the front door caved in.

May 1807

'Tristan de Montclair, what on earth would your mother say if she saw the state of your knees. School is for learning to read and write, not for fighting.' Brigitte stared at her charge in exasperation.

'I didn't start it,' Tris replied sullenly.

'Did you end it though, lad?' Antoine asked, hiding a grin.

'Oui, Papy, I put him straight on his backside.'

'Good lad.' Antoine gripped the boy's shoulder, ignoring his wife's disapproving look.

'The last thing we need is for Tristan to draw attention to himself,' Brigette scolded.

Antoine sighed at the familiar argument. 'We've been here over a year now, and there's been no sign of anyone sniffing around. He's a six-year-old boy. We can't wrap him in swaddling clothes.'

To his surprise, this time, Brigette didn't argue. 'I know,' she murmured. 'But I'd never forgive myself if anything happened to him.'

'Nothing will happen,' Antoine soothed. 'The attackers were likely *sans-culottes* chancing their luck, and the chateau's been empty for months. If they were interested in Tristan, they'd have tracked him down long before now.'

Brigitte sighed and nodded, pulling her apron off its hook and putting it over her head.

'Do you want anything from the market?' Antoine asked, relieved to change the subject.

His wife nodded, fishing a list out of her pocket. 'Take Tristan with you,' she suggested.

'I'd rather stay here,' the boy responded in a small voice. Brigitte looked at him narrowly. Clearly, it wasn't just his knees that were painful. Waving her husband off, she asked the lad if he wanted a glass of milk and a *Madelaine*.

Half an hour later, Tristan was licking his fingers after finishing off three of the small sponges and a large glass of milk. There were no other staff in the house. After the attack on Montclair, the only coin they had was the bag given to them just before they escaped. With care, Brigitte believed it would last them five years or so. But one of those years had passed already...

A sudden noise had Brigitte frowning. It couldn't be Antoine back already. It had sounded like glass smashing. Heart thudding, the former nursemaid told Tristan to stay put and ran out into the hall.

Seconds later, she reappeared, slamming the door behind her. For a second she didn't move, fear rendering her immobile. They'd been found.

Tristan stared at her in confusion. 'What's wrong, Tata?' he stuttered.

Without answering, Brigitte hurried to the window, moving to the side so she couldn't be seen. Lifting the curtain, she peered outside. Four men were standing between the house and the front gate. Biting her lip, she turned back to the now frightened boy. She realised they were trapped. There was no doubt the men were here to ensure that Philippe de Montclair's son did not live to claim his inheritance. Taking a deep breath, she walked calmly back to the table, crouching down in front of her charge.

'These are bad men, mon cœur,' she told him gravely, 'so we have to make sure they don't find you.' She held his shoulders gently. 'You're going to hide in the small space at the back of the larder – you know, the one you always go to when we play hide and seek?'

Tristan stared back at her solemnly before giving a small nod. 'It's important that you stay there until I come for you,' she continued, fighting a sob gathering in the back of her throat. 'If anyone calls for you other than me or Papy, you don't answer. You stay where you are, and you keep quiet. Do you understand, mon ange?'

Again, the boy nodded. 'Where are you going?' he added in a small voice as she pulled him to his feet.

'I will lead them away,' she responded with more confidence than she felt. 'Come, there's no time to waste. They will be here in moments.'

Seconds later, she gently but firmly pushed Tristan into the small cubby-hole at the very back of the larder where there was just enough room for him to sit. Watching her fearfully, he drew up his knees as she put her finger to her lips before shutting the small door. As darkness completely descended, he could hear her moving the large cask of salt in front to hide the opening.

Resting his head on his knees, rocking backwards and forwards, Tristan allowed the tears to fall silently. He heard faint shouting, crashing and then a short scream. He pushed his fist against his mouth, stifling a whimper. Then closer, a door opening and closing. More shouting... then nothing.

He didn't know how long he crouched there, but he knew it was a long time as he couldn't stop himself from peeing in his breeches. He hoped Tata wouldn't be too angry with him. Surely, she and Papy would come back soon?

And then he had the faintest whiff of smoke. With a low sob, he curled up into a ball on his side and somehow fell asleep.

Only to wake sometime later struggling to breathe, the air fetid and thick. Coughing, Tristan covered his nose and mouth with his arm. He was only six, but he knew he dared wait for Tata and Pape no longer. He had to get out.

Groaning with pain, the boy somehow manoeuvred himself onto his knees, then, with what remaining strength he had, he pushed at the door. At first it didn't move, then slowly, inch by inch, the cask of salt shifted, until finally, the opening was big enough for him to squeeze through.

The larder was filled with smoke, with the only relatively clear space directly above the floor. Crawling forward, Tristan pulled a cloth from around a wheel of cheese and, despite almost retching at the pungent stink, wrapped the material around his nose and mouth. Then, keeping his forehead on the relatively cool stone, he crawled on until his head finally hit the larder door.

Tears streaming from smoke and fear, Tris slid his hand upwards, feeling for the latch. It seemed to take hours, but eventually his fingers found it. Whimpering, he pushed at the bar until it lifted enough to unlatch the door.

As it swung open, without hesitating, Tristan crawled forward into hell.

Seventeen

May 1807

What he could see of the kitchen through the swirling smoke was mottled with black. Coughing through the cloth, he staggered to his feet, unsure which way to go as his sense of direction deserted him completely.

Eyes streaming, he turned round in a full circle before his eyes finally made out the door into the hall. Hurriedly, he took a step forward before suddenly noticing an orange glow around the edges. He couldn't go that way.

Almost choking now, he stumbled backwards just as flames began licking round the edges of the door. Seconds later he slammed against the edge of something hard. Turning, he realised it was the back door. Sobbing with relief, he fumbled with the catch. He didn't know if the bad men were outside – at the moment he didn't care. He just knew that if he stayed in the kitchen for one more moment, he would surely die.

At first the latch was stuck, the metal warping slightly as the temperature increased, then abruptly it gave, and yanking the door open, he fell out into the back garden. Pulling the stinking cloth from around his face, he lay where he'd fallen, drawing in great gulps of air. For a few stunned moments, he didn't move, then instinct took over. He had to find Papy.

Lurching to his feet, he looked round frantically but could see no one. Then, turning back towards the house, he recoiled in horror. The entire building was on fire. As he watched, an attic window exploded outwards, flames shooting out of the roof. Where was Tata?

Sobbing openly now, he staggered towards the secret gate and the tree-shrouded shortcut running along the edge of the river. He and Papy always used it when they went into town, although Tata would scold them and warn them about falling into the water.

As he pushed the gate open, he looked back once more, just as the roof collapsed. It was eerily silent until suddenly three men appeared. Instinctively, he took a step towards them, thinking they might help. They didn't look like bad men. But unexpectedly, they started laughing. His heart slammed against his ribs. Urgently, he turned back to the open gate, expecting them to spot him any second.

Stepping through, he hurriedly slammed it behind him and then started to run.

Whether he was still disoriented from inhaling too much smoke, or simply misjudged the edge, Tristan suddenly felt his left foot connect with nothing but fresh air. Arms flailing, he lurched to the side, hovering for a brief moment over the river before tumbling downwards towards the foaming water. With a panicked scream, he tried to put his hands out in front and ricocheted off the mossy bank, only to flip backwards, landing in the water with a splash. As he hit the shallow bottom, his head snapped back, straight onto a large rock, and everything went black.

Hours later, the boy came to. He lay on his back in the dark trying to remember how he'd got there, but try as he might, he simply couldn't remember. Faces flashed before his eyes, but none of them remained long enough for him to grasp. Finally, with a low moan, he managed to get onto his hands and knees and then onto his feet. Wobbling, he splashed towards the bank, where he collapsed again, drifting in and out of consciousness until dawn finally lit up the horizon.

Opening his eyes, the boy felt his stomach contract in hunger. Slowly sitting up, he looked around, but nothing felt familiar. He couldn't even remember his name. His stomach growled again, and in the way of all boys, his hunger overrode everything else. Ignoring his pounding head and his damp, filthy clothing, he climbed unsteadily to his feet, and went to look for something to eat.

Present day

Without taking his eyes off Tristan, Antoine Barbier tearfully explained that he and his wife Brigitte had been tasked with spiriting him away from the carnage unfolding in the chateau. At the time, it was believed that the much smaller, secluded house in Pontorson would provide a suitable refuge until it was deemed safe enough for the heir to the Marquisate to return home.

Unfortunately, however, that time never arrived. Just over a year later, whoever had attacked the Estate succeeded in locating their sanctuary, and, evidently determined to put an end to the only legitimate Montclair heir still living, they set the property in Pontorson alight with everyone in it.

Antoine's wife Brigitte had died in the flames, but Tristan's body was never found.

'I thought you were dead, boy,' Antoine whispered, his voice trembling. 'I looked everywhere for you, but there was no sign.' He shook his head, the tears falling unchecked as those around them looked on in silence.

Staring into the old man's distraught eyes, Tristan felt the first glimmerings of recognition. Pictures flashed up in his head, and this time, he sought to make sense of them.

A house, faces, smoke, a river, wet clothes. A man – *this* man - smiling at him with pride.

Suddenly, a word sprang into his head out of nowhere. Tristan's heart thudded as he reached out to take the old man's bent fingers in his. 'Papy,' he whispered, forcing back the lump in his throat...

The atmosphere at the inn that night was one of celebration. No one seemed in any doubt that Tristan was the missing heir, and in truth, the fact that Tris had recognised Antoine Barbier erased the last niggling doubt in Raphael's mind.

For the rest of the evening, Rafe watched the proceedings with cautious optimism. Rather than emptying as people returned to their homes, the bar gradually filled to bursting with people vying for Tristan's attention. Clearly, word was spreading of his arrival.

But it wasn't enough – the agent dared not rest on his laurels. They needed to get to the chateau as soon as possible. To be firmly in situ by the time Fontaine returned.

So he remained seated alone, taking mental notes of the local people's attitude towards Philippe's son's return. So far, everyone had appeared delighted, though Rafe knew that at least some of their euphoria was due to the liberal provision of free alcohol.

The problems would come tomorrow. At the moment, the drunken assumption was that Montclair's caretaker would be delighted to learn that the heir had returned home.

However, on waking in the cold light of day, there would be many who suspected the truth. They would fall into two categories. Those who would do what they could to protect Philippe de Montclair's son. And those who would happily profit from his betrayal.

Raphael's task now was to spot which was which.

Thinking on her grandfather's words, Henrietta carefully seated herself next to her mother. The two didn't speak, but clasped hands tightly, sharing a smile and a promise that the talking would come later. As they were served dinner, Henri divided her time between carefully observing both Raphael and Roseanna. She had no doubt that her cousin was delighted at Tristan's effusive welcome. However, Henrietta knew Rosie better than most and could clearly see the hint of worry in her eyes – likely down to an erroneous fear that once he was acknowledged as a marquis, he would no longer want to leg shackle himself to an introverted country miss. Of course, everyone who knew Tristan also knew such a concern was ridiculous.

The old Henrietta would have simply told her cousin not to be so deuced bacon-brained, but the recent conversation with her grandfather had caused Henri to think twice before making such sweeping statements. Indeed, the more she considered her own conduct, the more she realised what a peagoose she'd been.

Raphael Augustin was first and foremost an agent of the King. He was a *spy* who'd spent his entire adult life operating in the shadows. Why the devil would he even consider sharing vital information with a chit of a girl - no matter how astute he thought her?

Rafe had never tried to hide his ruthless, single-mindedness – and no one could argue that secretly putting his own man on board the *Fortune* had been both.

Everyone in their party might well have been outraged at what they saw as his betrayal, but if the agent had shared his actions with her father, and one of *Fortune's* long-time crew members had been unmasked as a traitor... In truth, Henri herself had been concerned about Roan Carew's ability to remain impartial when it came to his men. And despite his anger, her father realised it too.

She didn't know whether she and Raphael had any future at all, but she finally acknowledged that now wasn't the time to question it – no matter how much she wanted to. *Talk to him* her grandfather had advised, and Henrietta fully intended to do so – as soon as the whole havey cavey business was over.

They ate breakfast early the following morning. Rafe remained aloof from the rest of the party, his eyes constantly on the road outside, openly anxious about Fontaine's return.

News of Tristan's sudden appearance had travelled faster than expected and by lunchtime, the inn was again filled with local people seeking to take a look at the so-called lost heir. However, as Raphael had predicted, there was much more scepticism in the cold light of day.

Antoine Barbier spoke very little about their flight from Montclair on the night of the attack, preferring to talk about their time in Pontorson. Rafe had the feeling that he and his wife had been happy there. For much of the time, the old man sat close to Tristan, as if to reassure himself that he wasn't imagining things.

Raphael was acutely aware that they needed to be inside the Chateau before dark. Fontaine would likely return by noon on the morrow, and they had to make sure that Tristan was firmly ensconced before then.

Over lunch they decided that Rafe, Roan, Gabriel, Faith and Hope would accompany Tristan, while Henrietta and Roseanna remained at the inn with the Reverend, Percy, Dougal and Finn. While Raphael had initially been in favour of all the ladies remaining in the inn, both Faith and Hope had argued that their presence would add to the illusion that they were here merely as a favour to the new Marquis with no hidden agenda at all.

Faced with a possible mutiny, Rafe explained it was imperative they didn't all become trapped within the Chateau if they found themselves in the suds – a possibility that certainly couldn't be discounted.

'Well, I'm not rightly sure where you think the reinforcements are going to come from,' the Reverend declared matter-of-factly. 'You're not exactly knee-deep in military types here.'

'Ye speak fer yersel', Augustus Shackleford. We Scots be made o' sterner stuff than ye pigeon livered Sassenachs.' He stood up, fished out his bonnet and, plonking it on his head, launched into the opening bars of *Loch Lomond*. It would actually have been quite moving if Dougal hadn't had the voice of a strangled cat.

'Aye, anybodie wad hae tae be daft tae abide an' listen tae that noise. It be terrible,' Finn winced.

'Finn Noon, I believe you owe Dougal an apology,' Percy interjected sternly before an argument could ensue.

'It nae be ma fault Dougal cannae sing,' the boy protested.

'We will not be relying on you to provide the reinforcements,' Raphael countered through gritted teeth. Truly, he was dealing with idiots. 'You'll need to get yourselves back to the *Fortune* and tell Spalding. He will know what to do...' The agent paused and picked up his wine before adding, 'While there are no guarantees, it's always been my hope that Fontaine will see the futility of responding with violence when he discovers Tristan has reclaimed the Chateau. His punishment from those above him will be swift and brutal if he becomes involved in anything so public. My guess is they'll do nothing until the furore of Tristan's return has died down.'

'So, will this never end?' Roseanna asked, her voice trembling. 'Is Tris always going to be at the mercy of these men?'

Rafe shook his head decisively. 'We *will* bring them down. At the very least, Fontaine will know he is treading on very thin ice. My hope is that he'll realise his time is done. Whatever happens, he'll have failed – and those above him will not easily forgive that. I think he will try to negotiate.'

'So, will there be no retribution at all?' Tristan grated. 'This bastard had my parents murdered.' Roseanna laid her hand over her fiancé's, and he gripped it tightly.

Raphael looked at his countryman in sympathy. 'I cannot promise you Fontaine, my lord, but then he was never the one orchestrating your parents' death. He was simply the tool, and the truth is that we may well need to sacrifice the smaller fish to get at the bigger. But if Fontaine goes rogue, he'll have to give up those at the top, otherwise, he'll live the rest of his life looking over his shoulder.'

'Exactly like me then,' Tristan retorted bitterly.

Rafe grimaced and finished his wine. 'You are in an impossible position, yes, but I must remind you that it is not only you who stands to suffer if we do not catch these bâtards. God knows what plans and schemes they have in the works. They could destabilise not only the monarchy but also put our two countries back at war.'

After a brief silence, Tristan nodded his head slowly. 'You're right, my friend. Thank you for the timely reminder.' He gave a rueful grin before adding, 'I was well on the way to sucking my thumb there…'

Eighteen

As their carriages and drivers had been hired for the entire week, it was a simple matter to utilise two of them to take six of their party up to the Chateau. Loading the coaches with their belongings, however, was not quite so easily done.

'Dear God woman, how much luggage did you actually bring with you?' Gabriel quizzed his wife as he watched her trunk being loaded onto the carriage's imperial.

'I had no idea how long we would be away for,' Hope retorted, 'and I could hardly leave half my belongings at Redstone House.'

'Why, what did you think would happen to them?' her husband quizzed.

'Faith and I are remarkably similar in size,' Hope sniffed.

'I heard that,' her twin declared with mock outrage.

Hope turned round with an unrepentant grin. 'You know I love you, dearest, but if we're being honest with one another, your wardrobe leaves a lot to be desired.'

'There are more important things in life than clothes,' Faith snorted.

'Yes, hats,' Hope returned promptly.

'You sound like Aunt Tempy,' Henrietta laughed, knowing they were both trying to lighten the mood.

Hope gasped theatrically. 'You wound me to the quick, Henrietta Carew. And here you were, my favourite niece.'

'Well, you can't deny that Aunt Tempy's all the crack with the *ton*,' Rosie chimed in.

'You're absolutely right, dearest,' Faith responded with a sigh, 'but then your mother and I have always been chawbacons at heart.'

'Speak for yourself,' muttered Hope as Raphael came out to see what the fracas was. For a few seconds, they all stood like naughty children, causing the Frenchman to raise his eyebrows.

'I think Raphael has more important things on his mind that what is and isn't all the rage with the ton,' Roan announced, climbing down from the carriage.

'On the contrary,' Rafe declared drily. 'The comings and goings of the British aristocracy are of paramount importance to me...' He paused then, with a wry grin, added, 'and before you mutter to my back that I'm a complete philistine, I'll have you know that back in London, I'm considered a swell of the first stare.'

With the ladies staring at him as though he'd suddenly sprouted another head, Raphael gave them a broad wink that would have been the envy of any sailor before strolling back inside.

'Well, tare an' hounds, who'd have guessed the man has a deuced sense of humour,' Reverend Shackleford mused, staring after the agent in astonishment.

Henrietta felt a stab of regret as she watched Raphael vanish inside. She'd seen his sense of humour firsthand. On impulse, she walked into the inn after him, remaining in the doorway for her eyes to become accustomed to the dimness.

Ever since they arrived, the inn had been almost continually full, and today was no different. The innkeeper, at least, had been delighted at Tristan's return. She cast her eyes around the bustling bar, only to finally spot Raphael sitting alone near to the fire. He was studying what looked to be a map, and she took a disappointed step back, suddenly loathe to disturb him.

And then he looked up. Directly at her. While his expression never changed, Henrietta drew in her breath. She didn't know how, but she could feel his sense of isolation, his *need*. Unhesitatingly, she walked towards him. Whatever else she was to him would wait. Right now, she simply wanted him to know he had her support – no matter what had gone between them before.

And no matter what happened next.

Reaching the table, she sat down without waiting to be invited. He stared at her impassively, clearly waiting for her to speak. Twining her fingers together under the table, she gave a small cough.

'I wish to apologise for my outburst onboard the *Faith and Fortune,'* she faltered as he continued to watch her. 'I... while I do not condone the lie you told...' She paused and bit her lip. For pity's sake, she sounded like a self-righteous prig. 'The truth is, I have no concept of your world,' she went on hurriedly, 'and I realise I spoke without thought...' She cleared her throat before finishing in a rush, 'I do hope we can be friends again.'

For the longest moment he remained silent, and had there been a convenient hole, Henri would willingly have crawled into it. Then...

'Is that what we are – friends?' His voice was low, the tone giving nothing away, nevertheless, Henrietta felt an immediate tightening in her chest. She'd intended to wait until the danger was past. But what if it didn't pass? Instead, she met his eyes almost defiantly and shook her head.

He closed his eyes briefly, and when he opened them again, his eyes were no longer expressionless. Instead, they gave off a heat that had her drawing in her breath, her heart slamming against her chest. For the briefest of seconds, she fought the urge to push her chair back and run. The feelings rampaging through her body were too much.

But then he laid his hand over both of hers, gently prising them apart and replacing her entwined fingers with his own. He didn't speak, and she was glad. In truth, what was there to say?

'The carriages are ready to go.' The abrupt shout came from the doorway, and immediately a cheer went up in the bar. Rafe let go of her hand and got to his feet, quickly folding and tucking the map in his jacket. He had to fight his way outside as everyone was eager to see the Marquis begin the short journey to his ancestral home.

Rafe forced his way through the crowds to the front carriage, clearing a path for Tristan as the new Marquis shook hands, smiled and nodded. Roan was ready and waiting inside, and as soon as Tris was in, Raphael climbed up behind him and slammed the door shut, tapping on the roof in the universal signal to coach drivers everywhere. Gabriel, Hope and Faith were already installed in the second carriage and seconds later they moved off, their growing entourage unexpectedly following alongside and behind.

'Are they going to follow us all the way up to the Chateau?' Tristan speculated.

'It would be good if they did,' Rafe retorted with a tight smile. 'I've been told that there are no more than half a dozen servants and there doesn't appear to be any loyalty to Fontaine. I think while he hasn't actively abused the staff, neither has he inspired any devotion – and naturally they're all aware of Tristan's arrival.'

'We have a lot of bridges to build before Fontaine turns up,' Roan sighed. 'And at the end of the day, no matter how enthusiastic the locals are, we cannot allow them to get hurt in any potential crossfire.'

Rafe nodded. 'I still believe our greatest protection comes from word of mouth. We don't need fighters, we need gossips.'

Tristan glanced outside again. 'I've a feeling that whatever happens, this day will be spoken about for quite some time,' he mused thoughtfully.

Then, shaking his head, he gave his companions a tight grin. 'I never realised that suddenly becoming important would be such a bloody difficult thing to get used to.'

'Who said you're important?' Roan growled with a matching grin.

Sudden shouts put an end to their conversation. Raphael leaned out of the window. 'The gates are open, he told his companions. I've walked up three times since we arrived, and every time they've been closed.' He turned to Tristan. 'I'd like you to give a brief but impassioned speech to the crowd. Rousing, but not provoking, if that makes sense. Then send them home.'

'Naturally I have a pocketful of impassioned but not provoking speeches,' Tristan retorted drily. 'Do you think something's wrong?'

'I don't know,' Rafe answered, his eyes scanning the Chateau. 'But as Roan said, I'd rather these people were out of harm's way. A bunch of dead villagers are no use to us.'

'I think they'd most likely agree with you,' Tristan grimaced, taking hold of the door.

As he spoke to the villagers surrounding the carriage, Raphael and Roan kept their eyes on the Chateau. On the face of it, there appeared to be no activity, but that in itself made the Frenchman uneasy. 'He's actually pretty good,' Roan murmured, watching Tristan, his surprise evident in his tone.

'I think it's in the blood,' Rafe stated absently, still staring towards the open gates. After five minutes, there was a loud cheer, lots of clapping on the back as the villagers began drifting back down the road. Seconds later, the two carriages passed through the gate and entered the large courtyard.

'It's a pleasure to meet you, Monsieur le Marquis.' the young maid murmured, keeping her eyes downcast as she bobbed a curtsy

Tristan looked up at the old building, his heart thudding. Unexpectedly finding it difficult to swallow, he studied the conical-topped turrets, arched windows and the beautiful soft white limestone walls reflecting the watery sun. This was where he'd been born. Where he'd lived until he was five years old. He walked up the steps to where the maid still waited.

'You know who I am?' he commented as he reached her.

'Of course, Monsieur. The whole village knows of your arrival.'

Taking a deep breath, Tristan finally stepped through the great doors into the large reception hall – and stopped, looking round, sorrow flooding him.

In truth, the hall was in a sorry state. It was obvious that only the bare minimum had been spent on its upkeep. If the rest of the Chateau was in a similar condition, it was going to take a considerable amount of money to bring it back to its former glory.

Plainly, the coin in Montclair's coffers had long been directed elsewhere.

In addition to the maid, there were only three other servants, one of whom stared at him wordlessly, tears streaming down her face. A woman of at least seventy summers, her name, Tristan learned, was Madame Durand. She'd been the housekeeper for his parents. As he got closer to her, she tried to dip into a curtsy, but Tristan hurriedly took hold of her elbows before she fell over.

'I cannot believe it's you, Monsieur le Marquis,' she whispered brokenly. 'We all believed you dead. Monsieur Fontaine said you had been killed along with your parents.'

'Well, as you can see, Madame Durand, I am very much alive, and I am very happy to see you again.' He couldn't help wondering why the elderly servant was still residing in the chateau since she was clearly too old to work. Mayhap Fontaine had a compassionate side to him when he wasn't trying to murder the competition.

'Will you be staying... Monsieur le Marquis?' This time from a middle-aged woman whose tone was much more guarded. Raphael didn't miss her slight pause as she spoke the name.

'Naturally,' Tristan told her. 'This is my home.'

'It has been Monsieur Fontaine's home for some years now,' the woman answered.

Tristan looked around the bleak hall before raising his eyebrows. He did not comment, but the inference was obvious. By now he was flanked by Raphael and Roan, and behind him, Gabriel, Hope and Faith. His companions remained silent, knowing it was imperative Tristan stake his claim on the Chateau without their interference.

'I am truly grateful to Monsieur Fontaine for stepping in to take care of the Chateau,' Tristan continued steadily at length, 'but since he has been its caretaker, I'm sure you agree that it is not *actually* his home. I will of course be delighted to find him somewhere else to live after we have had the chance to go through the estate accounts.' He glanced obviously around the hall. 'May I ask where Monsieur Fontaine is now?'

The woman glanced over at the only other person who hadn't yet spoken – a man in his early thirties by Raphael's approximation. 'I believe Claude is visiting friends in St. Malo.'

Claude...

'And you are...?'

There was a sudden silence, then the man gave the barest inclination of his head 'Julien Dubois. I am Monsieur Fontaine's secrétaire.

'Ah, then you could well be just the man I need. While we wait for Monsieur Fontaine's arrival, you can show me where he keeps all matters pertaining to the estates. It will be tremendously helpful if we can get a head start on such mundane affairs.' He gave a broad smile, which was not returned. Indeed, Julien Dubois looked very much as though he would prefer to be anywhere other than where he was.

'I do not think we...' the secrétaire began, only for Tristan to hold up his hand.

'I'm certain Monsieur Fontaine values your opinion, but standing in the hall is not the place for me to hear it.' He turned to the middle-aged lady standing motionless. 'Madame, since you have not told me your name, I must beg your forgiveness if I seem rude. I presume you are the housekeeper?' He paused, looking at her inquiringly, giving her no option but to respond.

'I am the *Gouvernante*, yes,' she murmured after a moment. 'My name is Marie Laval.'

'Are there any other staff?' Tristan enquired.

'Only Thomas... Lefevre. He works outside.'

'Then would you please locate Thomas and request his assistance in bringing in the luggage?' Tristan was taking the utmost care to ensure his tone remained firm and pleasant, but his companions could see the signs of strain on his face. 'Then perhaps you could ensure that four rooms are made ready initially.'

'Initially?'

'That is what I said,' Tristan confirmed, his voice turning a little cooler. He was beginning to tire of their obvious prevaricating. 'Then, a pot of tea would be most welcome. Please direct us to the salon.'

It was another five minutes before the housekeeper showed them into a faded but surprisingly cosy room. The large fire crackling merrily in the huge fireplace gave testament to its regular use.

'Jeanne will bring your tea,' she murmured, before hurrying out of the room, shutting the door firmly behind her.

'Very impressive, Tris,' Roan declared as soon as they were alone. 'I truly didn't know you had it in you.'

'Once a nobleman, always a nobleman, obviously,' Tristan quipped with a faint grin.

'How long do you think we've got before Fontaine turns up with reinforcements?' Gabriel asked Raphael, watching the Frenchman peer out of the window.

'Whether he's taken in by Taffy's story or not, he now knows we're here,' Raphael retorted. 'Likely, he's already on his way back - with hard riding he could be here before dark ...' He stopped at the sound of a sudden thud against the door. Then another. Slowly, the latch was lifted, and the door started to open, before abruptly being flung back on its hinges.

As one, they got to their feet and turned towards the now wide-open door... just in time to see Taffy sink to his knees in the doorway. A second later, he fell face down onto the floor, revealing a large knife sticking out of the centre of his back.

Nineteen

'Do you think we should have heard something by now?' Rosie asked, putting down her éclair after only one bite.

'Ye gaun tae eat that?' Finn immediately quizzed her, his hand already hovering over the confection to prevent Dougal getting in there first.

'Finn,' snapped Percy. 'If your mother was here now, she'd be horrified at your manners. Anyone would think you haven't been fed at all today.'

'Aye, but that be two hours ago,' the boy wailed, 'an' right noo, ma belly dae think ma throat hae been cut.'

With a tired smile, Roseanna picked up the half-eaten cake and gave it to the ravenous boy. For once, Dougal merely narrowed his eyes and gave an indignant sniff as he watched Finn shoved the entire éclair into his mouth.

'I think this is one of those situations we're expected to use our own initiative,' Reverend Shackleford declared, rubbing his hands together.

Rosie favoured her grandfather with a suspicious look. Having only recently been on the receiving end of his more questionable *initiatives*, she was understandably wary.

'We dinnae want tae be askin' fer reinforcements afore the Frog gets tae speak wi' Fontaine,' protested Dougal.

'Absolutely not,' Augustus Shackleford agreed – a little too quickly in Percy's opinion. The curate eyed his superior narrowly.

'I hope you aren't planning to disregard Mr Augustin's instructions, Sir,' Percy quizzed him.

'You wound me, Percy.' the Reverend retorted. 'When have I ever failed to follow instructions?'

The rest of the table regarded him silently.

'The thing is, Grandpapa, you do have a tendency to act first and think later,' Henrietta murmured.

'I'll have you know that my razor-sharp instincts have saved the day on more occasions than I care to remember,' Augustus Shackleford protested huffily. 'The King himself declared me a national treasure....'

'Oh, you are,' Henri assured him. 'I mean, what would any of us do without you? What would *Flossy* do without you?' She was about to lay it on even browner, when suddenly the inn door opened, revealing a wheezing Antoine.

'Claude Fontaine is in the Chateau,' he panted, hanging onto the latch to keep himself upright. 'The scoundrel has taken Monsieur le Marquis and all your friends prisoner.'

Henrietta felt herself go cold all over. 'How do you know?' she demanded, climbing to her feet.

'The gates are shut, and he's stationed six of his men directly in front of them.' Antoine paused before finishing in an agonised whisper, 'They have *weapons*.'

'So much for deuced diplomacy,' the Reverend muttered.

'Be this when we're meant tae be usin' our own '*nishative*, Revren?' Finn asked.

~

No one spoke as Claude Fontaine stepped over the body of the sailor and sauntered over to an ancient cabinet. 'I admit you had me fooled,' he chuckled conversationally, laying his pistol on the top and pouring himself a large brandy, 'but at the end of the day, your ruse bought you little more than a few hours.' He turned and regarded them all unblinkingly. 'I was already on my way back when we bumped into *le marin*.'

Taking a sip of his brandy, he focused his attention on Tristan. 'You look very much like your father, nephew,' he mused. 'They told me you were his image.'

'Who told you?' Tristan queried, his voice carefully expressionless.

'It is of no import. Are you going to introduce me to your adopted family?'

Fontaine still believed his nephew was here purely to claim his inheritance. Rafe squeezed his hands into fists. Would Tristan pick up on it?

For a few moments, Tristan didn't respond, but just as his uncle's rapacious smile began to widen, he swept his hand towards the two couples.

'Meet my adoptive parents,' he expounded, with a wolfish grin of his own.

'My wife and I count ourselves most fortunate to have been part of Tristan's upbringing,' Roan enthused without hesitation.

'Indeed,' gushed Faith, 'and I'm certain my sister will tell you exactly the same.'

'All four of you were involved in bringing the boy up?' Fontaine commented, his eyes widening in studied disbelief.

'Oh, absolutely.' Hope beamed. 'He brought so much joy to our lives, didn't he, dearest?' She tucked her arm in Gabriel's, giving him an encouraging smile.

Gabriel nodded, directing an affectionate look towards Tristan.

Claude Fontaine's bewildered frustration was plain to see as he turned to Raphael. Clearly, their flippancy was having an effect. 'And where do you fit into this cosy arrangement, Monsieur?' he snapped, nodding towards the corpse lying in the doorway. 'I must warn you that our mutual friend was surprisingly helpful – while he still had a tongue to speak with, of course.'

Rafe felt his heart contract as he feverishly thought back to the conversation with Taffy. At no point had he mentioned exactly what his role was. Fontaine was fishing.

'Then you already know that Tristan and I have been friends since school,' he acknowledged. 'I was the one who first saw the portrait of his birth father. That was how this odyssey began.' He looked over at the unfortunate Taffy. 'I must confess, we were not expecting violence. What did the man do to warrant such a grisly end?'

'Lied,' answered Fontaine shortly. He slammed his empty glass down on the cabinet and picked up his pistol. 'I think this charade has gone on long enough. You might be here to claim your inheritance, but unfortunately, I am not ready to let you have it. Surely you did not expect to walk in here and simply claim it for yourself?' His voice turned sneering.

Rafe gritted his teeth. He was well aware that the others were waiting on his lead. Fontaine had made no effort to hide his pistol, but in truth, he must have known he couldn't overpower all of them. Obviously, he had men waiting within earshot. How far was the bâtard willing to go? He would never get away with killing all of them. Not now so many people knew of the Marquis's return.

But as he looked into Claude Fontaine's feverish, almost glittering eyes, Raphael realised that the man was swiftly moving beyond rational thought, and the one possibility he hadn't considered before that second was that Fontaine might be deranged...

Was now the time to tell him they were aware of his treasonous activities? Doing so could quite easily push him over the edge, but it might also goad him into giving them a name.

Did he dare take such a risk? In the past he wouldn't have hesitated, but up until now, he'd never had anything – or anybody - to lose. That was what had made him so dangerous. Now, contrary to all expectations, he actually had people he cared about, and the very fact that he was dithering made him equally dangerous.

These thoughts and more raced through Raphael's mind in seconds, but just as he opened his mouth to speak, he saw the wall behind Claude Fontaine suddenly move.

'Thunder an' turf, what a deuced bag of moonshine,' Reverend Shackleford groaned.

'I think now's the time to fetch reinforcements from the *Fortune*, Sir,' Percy stated urgently.

'But if Fontaine is holding them prisoner, their lives are in danger now,' Roseanna reasoned, trying hard to force back her panic. 'It could be hours before help arrives.'

'The Frog didn't think this one through, did he?' muttered the Reverend, giving Henrietta a pointed look.

'Dae ye reckon the bampot be aff his heid, Revren?' Finn questioned, his voice a mixture of trepidation and excitement.

'Aye, ah fear the lad be right,' Dougal chimed in. 'Ah'll goan an' fetch help.'

'Is this you being helpful, Dougal Galbraith, or deuced chuckleheaded?' the Reverend growled.

'It be me bein' bloody sensible,' the Scot muttered under his breath, before adding in a louder voice, 'An' o' course bein' a descendant o' the Galbraiths o' Culloden, ah be a natural on the back o' a horse.'

Both the Reverend and Percy looked at him doubtfully. 'Hae ye niver seen a Scot ride in tae battle?' Dougal asked with a very creditable swaggering grin.

'Err... not recently,' Percy confessed.

'*Ha*,' Dougal roared, making them all jump – including Flossy, who gave a low growl. 'Ready yersels fer a sight ye'll niver forget,' he continued, climbing to his feet. 'Marvel as ah be one wi' th'orse.'

With that, he picked up his cloak, and strode to the entrance. Throwing open the door, he turned back, swirling the cloak over his shoulders with a flourish before stepping through and slamming the door behind him – only to reappear a couple of seconds later to ask where the nearest horse actually was...

Another ten minutes passed by the time they'd established that the only horse owned by the innkeeper was at least thirty years old and unlikely make it fifty yards down the road, let alone to Perros-Guirec and back, and another ten minutes before they persuaded the disappointed Dougal to take one of the two remaining carriages.

Watching him finally disappear into the distance, the Reverend breathed a relieved sigh at the reprieve. Unfortunately, the sentiment was not shared by his remaining companions.

'We can't simply sit here twiddling our thumbs until Dougal gets back with reinforcements,' Henrietta commented. 'That's if he even comes back. I think Rosie's right. We need to do something now.'

'Dae we rescue 'em like the knights in a book, Da?'

'I don't think we can march up to the Chateau and rescue them from under the blackguard's nose, son,' Percy responded with a sigh. 'They'll see us while we're still half a mile away.'

'Not if you go through the tunnels,' Antoine interjected.

The Reverend raised his eyebrows. 'What deuced tunnels?'

'They've been here since Robespierre's time,' Antoine went on. 'The old Marquis wanted a way for the family to escape quickly.' He shook his head sadly, before adding, 'I don't reckon he thought he'd be sending his only son through 'em though.'

'You escaped with Tristan through these tunnels?' Augustus Shackleford quizzed him, the first stirrings of excitement in his voice. 'Where do they lead to?'

'There's one goes from the library and one from the second salon. Both meet up and lead into the woods beyond the town.'

'And you don't think Fontaine knows about these?' the Reverend questioned.

'The Marquis never told anybody about 'em – just kept it within the family. That's how we were able to smuggle young Tristan out.'

'And since then?' Henrietta asked. 'Do you think anyone's discovered them?'

Antoine paused, his brow furrowed. 'I can't imagine how or when. Monsieur Fontaine has never spent much time at the Chateau. Madame Durand, the old housekeeper, is always telling me he's off on some business or another.'

'Where did you say the tunnels come out?' Roseanna asked.

'Not half a mile from here. I can take you all if you want. There's only one way in, so you can't get lost. You'll know you're underneath the Chateau when the walls turn into limestone.'

'You said they originate in the library and in the salon,' Reverend Shackleford clarified. 'How do we know which tunnel to take?'

'Once you're under the Chateau, you'll come to a fork. If you want the library, take the right one. For the salon, it's left…' he stopped, puckering his brow. 'Or is it the other way round? It was a long time ago I was last in 'em.'

'But even if we manage to get all the way into the house, what can we possibly do?' Percy argued.

'We'll niver ken wi oot tryin', Da. That be wat ye tell me.'

Percy looked at his son's excited face – almost exactly like the Reverend's and sighed. Truly, the lad would be the death of him.

'There's no time to waste, Percy my man,' the Reverend declared. 'It'll be like old times – just me and you venturing into danger and saving the day...'

'You're not venturing anywhere without me and Rosie,' Henri proclaimed, the mulish expression on her face daring her grandfather to argue.

'Me too,' Finn chimed in. 'An' dinnae forget Flossy.'

In the end, it took them half an hour to reach the tunnel entrance, mostly because Antoine had forgotten where it was located, and by the time he finally got his bearings, he looked ready to keel over.

The entrance was cleverly hidden behind a prolific tangle of vines growing down from a mossy bank, and after pointing at the faint *M* carved into the stone on one side, the old man sat down on a large rock, mopping his brow. 'After I've had a breather, I'll go back to the village and spread the word,' he wheezed.

'Excellent idea,' Reverend Shackleford agreed, patting the old man on the back. 'Rile 'em up, Antione lad.' Privately he couldn't help wondering if the old fellow would actually make it back to the village, let alone indulge in a spot of rabble-rousing.

They remained with him until they were sure he wasn't going to collapse on the spot. 'Dae ye reckon he'll peg oot afore he gets back tae the village, Revren?' Finn asked in a loud whisper.

'I've no idea, Finn my lad,' the Reverend whispered back, equally loudly. 'But better he does it there rather than here. Nothing says suspicious tunnel like a dead body stuck outside the deuced entrance...'

Finally, after fishing about in his cassock for the tinderbox, the Reverend lit the oil lamp they'd borrowed from the innkeeper. Then, turning to look at the tangle of vines, he muttered, 'Right then...'

'Do you think it's safe?' Henrietta asked as she watched him pull the creepers back and hold up the lamp to peer inside.

'I reckon there might be a few spiders,' the clergyman muttered as he stepped through, only to be immediately swallowed by the gloom until all she could see was a bobbing light.

'What kind of spiders?' Roseanna hissed as she followed Henrietta in after him.

'Big ones...' The Reverend's chuckle was muffled in the dank space.

'Dae ye let me keep one, Da? Like a pet mebbe?' Finn said over his shoulder as his father brought up the rear.

'Flossy would eat it,' came Percy's prompt reply. He was finally beginning to realise that a direct no came with its own problems.

Tucked in the boy's arms, the little dog's pricked up on hearing her name. 'Ugh, that be bowkin,' was all Finn muttered before lapsing into silence - likely contemplating the strategic measures involved in keeping a pet spider.

Twenty sweaty and grimy minutes later, they were just beginning to wonder whether Antoine had sent them into the wrong tunnel, when the Reverend suddenly stopped. 'Does that wall look different to you?' He held up the lamp as they turned to inspect the tunnel wall.

'It's limestone,' Percy confirmed. 'I think we must be finally under the chateau. Please don't be tempted to do anything foolish, will you, Sir.?'

'Don't be such a deuced chucklehead, Percy,' the Reverend grumbled, starting forward again. 'This is just like old times. The two of us throwing a rub in the way of a good-for-nothing scoundrel's nefarious scheme.'

Unfortunately, since the curate had heard virtually the same sentence during every other totty-headed idea his superior had dreamed up, it didn't provide quite the inspiration the Reverend might have hoped for...

'Thunder an' turf...' Augustus Shackleford stopped a few moments later and held up the lamp. The passage was completely blocked by rubble.

‘We can’t turn back,’ Rosie declared, her voice desperate. ‘Who knows what horrible things that awful man might be doing to them all, right this second.’ Without answering, Reverend Shackleford swung his lamp, revealing another tunnel snaking off to the left.

‘I’d wager this one goes to the salon,’ the Reverend enthused. ‘Come on, we’re going to put a stop to this varmint once and for all...’

Twenty

'Antoine never mentioned that the way into the salon was via a deuced ladder a mountain goat would have had difficulty scaling.'

'Could there be another way in?' Percy queried, studying the door, which unfortunately happened to be ten feet off the ground.

'Well, as much as I'd like to say otherwise. I really don't think there is,' Reverend Shackleford sighed.

'Why just a ladder?' Roseanna asked. 'Anybody trying to get in or out is likely to risk a broken leg or worse.'

'Perhaps that's the point,' Percy suggested. 'If anyone who didn't know the tunnels tried to escape that way, they'd get a nasty shock when their foot stepped out into nothing.'

'But what about those trying to get in?' Henrietta shook her head 'Do you really think it leads into the salon?'

'There's only one way to find out,' the Reverend affirmed. 'Come on, Percy, lad, you're going to have to give me a bit of a push.'

Almost exactly the same words had last been uttered to Percy during their tree-climbing incident outside the Earl of Cottesmore's house all those years ago, and in truth the curate's nose had never been the same since...

After rubbing his hands together, the Reverend lifted one foot off the ground. Unfortunately, there was still a sizeable gap to the first rung of the ladder.

'Perhaps Rosie or I might be better to go up,' Henrietta suggested as their grandfather hopped up and down on his left foot in an attempt to get his right foot that bit higher.

'Certainly not,' Augustus Shackleford puffed. 'How the devil are either of you going to overpower the blackguard? I just need a bit of a step up. Come on Percy.'

'I'm not sure, that's...'

'Right then, I'll take off me frock, so I've got a bit more movement.' The Reverend pulled off his cassock, handed it to a riveted Finn, and abruptly began hopping from foot to foot. 'To limber up,' he explained breathlessly. Unfortunately, the bouncing motion swiftly began to have an adverse effect on his waterworks - not helped by the fact that his breeches were just a tad on the snug side. After only a few seconds, he stopped and grabbed hold of the ladder, wondering whether Percy might possibly have a convenient chamber pot stashed somewhere under his cassock. But since the curate weighed little more than a wet lettuce, it only took a quick glance to reveal the absence of any unidentified protuberances.

Reverend Shackleford gritted his teeth. There was no time to waste.

'Right, Percy, stop dithering and give me a quick shove,' he ordered urgently. 'Once I'm on that deuced ladder, the Frog's as good as finished.'

Finn's muttered, 'Which one?' was largely ignored.

With a grimace, Percy succumbed to the inevitable, and positioning himself directly next to the ladder, he bent down and cupped his hands.

After a few tries, Reverend Shackleford succeeded in getting his foot into the makeshift cradle, then, with a grunt, he grabbed hold of the ladder above his head. 'On my mark, Pe...' he started, only to give a startled yelp as he suddenly shot upwards. On the plus side, he managed to hook his arm around the rung of the ladder, but on the minus side, his feet were left dangling in midair...

While sheer panic fortunately lessened the Reverend's urgent need of a chamber pot, it did nothing for his ladder climbing skills, forcing Percy to hurriedly place a hand under each of his superior's buttocks for the second time in his life. This time, unfortunately, though he might vehemently deny it, there was no doubt that Augustus Shackleford had put on weight.

His arms trembling with strain, Percy stared upwards in horror, his entire life flashing before his eyes, as the Reverend's more than generous posterior came inexorably closer. In fact, he'd just resorted to praying when, at long last, Augustus Shackleford finally managed to get his foot on the bottom rung of the ladder...

Silence ensued, broken only by panting as both men contemplated their mortality.

'Ah reckon if ye didnae want tae be God botherers anymore, ye and the Revren'd be crackin' in the circus, Da.'

Raphael froze, keeping his eyes carefully on Fontaine while taking note of the panel that was opening inch by inch no more than six feet behind the caretaker's head. He dared not look over to see whether any others of their party were aware, but simply kept his eyes on Fontaine as the Frenchman ranted.

Seconds later, Reverend Shackleford's head cautiously appeared through the narrow opening and, for some strange reason, it was only a foot from the floor. Raphael felt as though he'd stumbled into a bizarre dream. What the bloody hell was the priest doing inside the walls of Chateau Montclair?

Without appearing to, Raphael watched Augustus Shackleford stick his head out further, and suddenly begin waving. The frantic movements slowly pushed the door ever wider until Rafe realised the whole of the clergyman's bottom half was somehow below the threshold of the door. For one incredulous second, he wondered whether the Reverend was floating, having finally gone on to receive his heavenly reward - then Finn's head popped up beside him.

'Can we assume you are denying Tristan de Montclair his birthright?' Raphael said coldly but loudly in an effort to drown out the whispered argument now coming from the hole in the panel.

If Rafe was looking to goad their captor into doing something stupid, he'd unknowingly chosen exactly the right words. Indeed, Claude Fontaine's response was immediate and chillingly unhinged.

With a scream, the fictitious caretaker lifted his arm and pointed the pistol directly at the King's agent. His hand wavering wildly, he yelled, 'Why should he have it? Why should he have *any* of it? *I* was the eldest son. Me. *Montclair is rightfully mine.*' The gun swung towards Tristan, just as Finn managed to clamber up onto the floor of the salon. Sprinting towards Fontaine, the boy threw himself to the floor, sliding the last few feet on his side and crashing directly into the back of the Frenchman's legs. With a yell, Fontaine fell backwards, the pistol firing wildly towards the ornate ceiling.

At the same moment, Rafe threw himself at the traitor, grappling for the pistol, just as the Reverend appeared, holding a large vase in the air which he brought down on the traitor's head with a satisfying crack – immediately after which he looked desperately at Tristan and asked the location of the nearest privy.

The commotion naturally brought Claude Fontaine's cut-throats running into the room. On seeing their employer unconscious on the floor, three of them raised their weapons.

'Don't be bloody fools,' Tristan snapped, facing them. 'At the moment, you have no blood on your hands. The moment that changes, the only thing awaiting you will be the guillotine.'

For a second none of them moved, then as one, they laid their muskets on the floor and stepped back, just as the sound of shouting reached them from outside. Striding to the window, Roan watched disbelievingly as approximately two hundred villagers stormed the Chateau gates.

Turning back to Tristan he nodded his head towards the window and chuckled, 'It looks as though you are important after all...'

To a man, Claude Fontaine's armed guards had vanished within half an hour of their employer's detainment. Tristan's uncle had been placed under house arrest along with Marie Laval and Julien Dubois, with sailors from the Fortune guarding them until Raphael could begin their formal questioning the following day.

Dinner that evening was held in the Chateau's dining room. With the scarred table and threadbare furnishings, it was hardly the grand return Tristan might have hoped for, but nevertheless, the mood around the table was light. While the new Marquis still had to be formerly recognised, missives would be sent to the appropriate legal authorities over the coming days, and since Tristan was the image of his father, Rafe didn't anticipate any problems – in that area at least.

Since they were down to a single maid and definitely no cook, the villagers had taken it upon themselves to ensure the returning Marquis's homecoming was at least as comfortable as possible. By the time they sat down to eat, fires burned in every grate, and clean sheets made up on every occupied bed. The food was simple, but delicious - a common Breton staple similar to a pancake, called a galette. Each one was filled to bursting with ham, cheese and eggs, which everyone consumed with relish, including Flossy.

Throughout the meal, no one mentioned the chateau's state of disrepair, though the amount of coin given over to its upkeep had clearly been minimal. Naturally, the most pressing problem was the uncertainty over whether there was actually any money left in the coffers, or whether the entire Montclair fortune had been used to fund Fontaine's treasonous activities. Fontaine had previously declared the money missing, and they'd yet to see any evidence that his claim was false.

After dinner, the entire party gathered together in the large drawing room, or as the maid called it, *la salle de reception*. It was very evident that the room hadn't been in use for many years - likely since Tristan's parents had been alive - but the villagers had worked hard to make it comfortable. The entire room had been thoroughly cleaned and swept and liberally sprinkled with sweet-smelling herbs to take away the underlying smell of damp. Fires now burned merrily in the two huge fireplaces, and additional furniture had been moved from other rooms to ensure everyone had a place to sit.

Tristan and Roseanna sat close together, though both bore identical expressions of equal parts elation and apprehension. Restoring such a large building was not for the fainthearted, and wouldn't be possible at all if there truly was no money.

But at least Rosie's ridiculous concern that her fiancé would discard her had been entirely put to bed. Indeed, Henrietta wondered wryly whether the boot might now be on the other foot, since her cousin might not wish to spend years helping with such an ambitious renovation project. But knowing Roseanna, Henri didn't think she would balk at the challenge, and one might argue that young blood was exactly what the chateau needed to bring it back to life. Doubtless they would receive support from the entire extended Shackleford clan.

Henri found herself watching Raphael throughout the rest of the evening. He seemed relaxed, but she'd become attuned to him enough to recognise the tautness of his shoulders, the periodic clenching of his fingers, and his constant glances towards the door. She was aware that his man Jacob was no longer in the chateau and guessed he'd been tasked with relaying messages back to England.

Tomorrow, Fontaine would be questioned. Henrietta knew what that meant, and while she recoiled at the idea of violence, she was worldly enough to realise that Raphael dared not walk out of the interrogation room without the information he needed. The lives of too many people depended on it.

This was the man she'd fallen in love with...

Biting her lip, Henrietta bent her head, abruptly swamped with fear. How on earth could they ever carve out a future together? They came from different worlds. Her heart thudded even as her mind wrestled with the question. And then she looked up. Straight into Raphael's eyes. He looked at her steadily, but his eyes were filled with anguish, and Henri realised he knew exactly what she was thinking. Fighting the urge to cry, Henrietta got to her feet and addressed the room in general. 'I hope you'll forgive me,' she managed round the sudden lump in her throat, 'but it's been a long day and I find myself unable to keep my eyes open.' She turned to her grandfather. 'Would you like me to take Flossy out quickly to do her business before I retire?'

Clearly, thinking it gave him time for one more brandy, the Reverend happily gave his consent. Flossy, of course, didn't need to be told twice, and promptly jumped off her master's lap and trotted over to Henrietta. 'Ah'll come wi' ye, Miss Henri,' Finn offered enthusiastically, jumping to his feet.

'I think you've had enough excitement for one day, lad,' Percy countered. 'You're going nowhere but your bed.'

Before the boy had a chance to protest, Raphael climbed to his feet. 'Allow me to accompany you, Miss Carew,' he said with a polite smile. 'I confess I'm ready to turn in myself but could certainly do with a little air beforehand.'

Henri glanced over at her parents. Both were regarding her speculatively, but neither voiced any objection to the King's agent accompanying her. Heart pounding, she murmured her thanks and went to fetch her cloak, Flossy at her heels.

Minutes later, they were outside in the large courtyard. The gates were still being manned by several of Fortune's crew on the off chance that not all of Claude Fontaine's hired soldiers had fled and Raphael suggested they walk towards the gardens to the side of the house. Feeling particularly exposed with all the windows at the front of the house, Henri was happy to comply.

As they walked, Flossy nosing happily alongside, Rafe asked her about the trip through the tunnels. Not sure whether he was simply making conversation or really needed to know, Henrietta endeavoured to give him a full account, although halfway through, her description inevitably turned humorous. 'I must confess, I thought Percy done for when Grandfather nearly fell on him', she chuckled, 'and then, when Grandpapa finally got to the top of the ladder and Finn climbed up too, I thought he might be about to have an apoplexy.' She shook her head. 'Poor old Percy, I think he's been dragged into many such capers over the years. I don't know why he's put up with it. In truth, my uncles have threatened to swing for Grandpapa on several occasions.'

Rafe raised his eyebrows. 'I can imagine being related to such an... enthusiastic individual has provided unique challenges,' he murmured.

Henrietta glanced sideways at him. Incredibly, just minutes alone in his company and her earlier fears were already beginning to evaporate. She felt a sudden faint hope. 'I believe interfering is the word you're looking for,' she quipped. 'Or nosey, meddlesome, too inquisitive for his own good – he's been called all of those things and a lot worse besides.'

Rafe laughed. 'A living legend,' he returned drily.

'Not for much longer if he continues meddling the way he does.' Henrietta's grin faded as she shook her head before adding thoughtfully, 'But, you know, the one thing I admire about Grandpapa is his belief in himself and be damned what anyone else thinks.'

'He has God on his side,' Raphael reminded her.

'True,' she smiled. 'But earlier today I accused him of acting first and thinking later.' She stopped and turned towards Raphael. 'Perhaps that's not always such a bad thing,' she murmured, her heart hammering as she looked up at him. 'If one insists on waiting for every piece to be in place, then one could be waiting forever...'

In answer, Rafe lifted his hand and traced his fingers down her cheek. The merest touch, but it sent shivers through her that had nothing to do with the cold. She lifted her own hand to touch his opposite cheek, revelling in the faint roughness under her fingers, and slowly, achingly, his mouth came down on hers, touching, tasting, searching. But before the kiss had the chance to deepen, Raphael groaned and lifted his head, his dark gaze clinging to hers in the muted light.

'Do you believe that two people who have led completely different lives can be together?' he questioned, his voice hoarse. 'Is it enough that I love you?'

For a second, Henrietta was too full up to answer, but finally she managed a shaky laugh as she whispered back, 'I think my entire family are living proof of that.'

Twenty-One

The jubilation of the day before was undeniably missing at breakfast the next morning as the reality of what still hadn't been resolved arrived with the cold light of day. It didn't help that Dougal spent the entire time complaining that his 'heid be aboot tae burst,' while the Reverend looked as though he'd just been dug up. Naturally, the empty brandy bottles told their own story.

The morning passed agonisingly slowly for Henrietta. She was relieved to know that her father and Uncle Gabriel were sitting in with Raphael during the interrogation – not because she feared what the King's agent would do left to his own devices, but more what he would *not* do after his declaration of the night before.

Raphael Augustin had told her that he loved her. The tone in which he'd said it was more akin to a confession that he had some incurable disease, but Henrietta wasn't about to be picky.

His admission might not have been couched in flowery language, but to Henrietta it meant far more than just three words. It meant there was a possibility of a future between them. How that future would look was anybody's guess. But the knowledge that her feelings were reciprocated was enough. Somehow, they would make it work.

Today, however, there was no room for sentiment...

Halfway through the morning, Madam Durand came looking for Tristan. Initially, the new Marquis was less than inclined to speak with the old housekeeper, preoccupied as he was in trying to make some sense of his uncle's almost nonexistent accounting. When Madame Durand refused to speak with anybody else, however, he relented and invited her into his study.

Half an hour later, Tristan came out, just as Raphael, Roan and Gabriel finished their interrogation.

Roan immediately headed to the brandy decanter on the sideboard. 'May I?' he asked Tristan. The new Marquis nodded. 'It's yours as long as there's some left,' he quipped.

'Fontaine seemed genuinely surprised that we were aware of the *Revisionists*,' Rafe stated, accepting the brandy. 'As we suspected, he actually believed that Tristan was here solely to reclaim his inheritance.' He paused, shaking his head. 'I'm beginning to think he was actually a very small fish in the pond and his only usefulness was continued access to the Montclair name and fortune.'

'He's admitted the involvement of Lord Pemberton,' Gabriel announced tiredly, 'but claims he has no proof.' The Viscount's distaste with the whole procedure was obvious as he added, 'In truth, I find it hard to believe that Pemberton's a traitor. He's a decorated Admiral for God's sake. He and his wife were guests at our wedding.'

'Without proof, we have nothing anyway,' Raphael grated. 'If he's cornered, Pemberton will only deny it – and it's a felon's word against that of a peer.'

'What if Finn's able to identify him?' Faith asked.

'An orphan who's the adopted son of a country curate,' Rafe answered bluntly.

Beyond giving permission for the brandy, Tristan had so far contributed little to the conversation. On his lap he held a leather-bound book, which he was studying intently.

'What's that you have, Tris?' Roan quizzed him at length - just as Tristan uttered an exclamation.

Looking up, the Marquis held out the book. 'My father's diary,' he explained hoarsely. 'He gave it to Madame Durand the day he died with instructions to give it to me when she saw me again...' He stopped abruptly and covered his face with his hands, unexpectedly overcome with emotion for a man he couldn't even remember. Roseanna laid a hand on his arm but gave him the space he needed to grieve, while everyone else waited silently until he was ready to go on.

'It seems my father had long suspected his brother's treachery,' Tristan managed at length, 'so he transferred the Montclair fortune to England to prevent Claude accessing it.' He paused, then gave a sardonic laugh that was almost a sob. 'Here is my father's last entry...

"God help me, the money is in trust with Admiral Lord Pemberton, the very man who has conspired against me with my own brother..."'

The silence was absolute.

'There's more,' Tristan went on, his voice stronger now. 'An envelope containing dates, payment records and letters my father discovered between Fontaine and Pemberton. Everything you need to see the bastard swing.' He held out the envelope to Raphael. The King's agent took it without speaking.

As always, it was left to the Reverend to say what everyone else was thinking. 'Well then, we'll just have to pray old Pemberton hasn't spent the deuced lot in the meantime.'

Fortuitously, the Duke and Duchess of Blackmore were still in London when the urgent missive arrived naming Lord James Pemberton as the leader of the *Revisionists*. Nicholas immediately contacted his brother-in-law, Jamie. As a magistrate, Jamie Fitzroy had been very much involved in the investigation of Etienne Babin and would set the wheels in motion for Pemberton's arrest before the peer had a chance to flee the country.

The Duke's next stop was naturally the King. He didn't have to wait long. Lord Castleton, his majesty's chief Gentleman's Usher, was showing him into the King's chamber within the hour, and by the end of the day, Pemberton had been taken into custody and charged with treason.

The peer's questioning had gone on long into the night. While he readily admitted to syphoning funds from the Montclair coffers in his charge, he denied using the coin to support the *Revisionist* cause, maintaining he knew nothing of the conspiracy. Unfortunately for Pemberton, the evidence collected by Philippe de Montclair was for the most part unarguable, and despite the lack of a confession, it seemed certain he would face the gallows.

At long last, due in no small part to assistance from beyond the grave, the *Revisionist* Conspiracy had finally been laid to rest

What was left of the Montclair fortune was returned to its new Marquis and, though Pemberton had used it carefully, taking great care to cover his tracks, Tristan feared there wouldn't be much left after the chateau had been restored. That said, the estate ledgers going back nearly a century were a good indication of just how fertile the land surrounding the estate had always been. In fact, it had traditionally supported the family through the leaner times, and Tristan saw no reason it couldn't do so now. The fact that the land had remained fallow for so long would ultimately prove a good thing, though, as Tristan commented drily, he was unlikely to be playing *gentleman farmer* any time soon...

Since both the Marquis and the soon-to-be Marquise were understandably eager to begin the renovations to their future home, Gabriel reluctantly gave his permission for the wedding to be brought forward. After everything that had happened, it was to be a small, intimate family affair at Northwood within the month – although the words *small* and *intimate* were not generally used when referring to Shackleford family gatherings...

~

'When are you going to tell me exactly what's wrong, darling?' Faith finally managed to corner her daughter in the library a full week after their return – not an easy feat since Henrietta had spent nearly every waking moment in her bedchamber.

Though Faith had held back in the hope that Henri would choose to confide in her, she could no longer bear to watch her usually ebullient daughter fade into the wallpaper. 'You look dreadful, sweetheart,' her mother went on, resolutely, 'and we both know this can't go on. Your father is on the verge of calling Raphael Augustin out...'

She left the sentence hanging, watching Henri's reaction carefully. She wasn't disappointed. The emotions flitting across the young woman's face veered from disbelief to horror to downright misery, and seconds later she burst into tears.

'Oh, sweetheart,' Faith murmured, taking the sobbing woman into her arms. 'Do you think your father and I are blind? We guessed you were developing feelings for Raphael Augustin. Please tell me he hasn't harmed you in any way?'

Henrietta shook her head vehemently but did not speak. Taking a deep breath, her mother ploughed on. 'I have to confess I've found the man nigh on impossible to read, but still, your father and I were very much under the impression he returned your feelings. That's the only reason we did not act. Were we wrong?' She guided Henrietta to the large chair by the fire and knelt at her feet, a sudden thought occurring. 'You are not with child, are you, dearest?'

Henrietta looked at her mother incredulously through her tears. 'No,' she managed, dashing at her eyes. The question had the desired effect, however, and her crying dwindled to sniffing as she accepted her mother's kerchief to mop up her face. After another five minutes, she gave a sad chuckle. 'No, I am not with child,' she repeated with a sigh. 'In fact, chance would have been a fine thing.'

Taken aback at her daughter's directness, Faith rocked back on her heels. In truth, she had no answer to that. In fairness, it was almost heartening to know Henrietta was a chip off the old block...

'You look like a fish, Mama,' Henri observed drily and seconds later, both women unexpectedly dissolved into giggles, breaking the barrier that had somehow come between them.

In between sniffs, Henrietta finally confessed everything to her mother. 'While we were still in the chateau, Raphael admitted that he loves me, Mama,' she admitted finally, 'and though I've heard nothing from him since we returned, I don't believe he was playing me false.'

'He has had much to deal with,' Faith commented gently.

Henrietta nodded. 'I know. And I also know that I sound like a whingeing child. But I'm not, Mama. I'm fully aware of just how difficult it will be for him to extract himself from the world he's been in for so long...' She stopped and gave a despairing shrug before adding, 'I'm just so afraid that as long as we're apart, he'll forget why he wanted to leave it.'

With a sigh, Faith climbed to her feet and went to ring for some tea. 'The wedding is in two weeks time,' she declared, sitting in the chair opposite. 'He will be there. You can write to him in the meantime, but – and I hate to say this, sweetheart, but I feel I must – I believe you *both* need some time apart to think. Your relationship has had no chance to develop normally...' She paused and gave a small laugh. 'In truth, it was exactly the same for your father and me. We had some time without each other after the danger had passed, and I...' She stopped again as the door opened to admit Mrs Bellamy carrying a tray of tea and biscuits.

Sensing there was more to her mother's speech than just 'wait,' Henrietta watched impatiently as the housekeeper poured the tea. Fortunately, Faith waited only until the door was closed before continuing.

'As I said, the wedding is two weeks away, and Raphael Augustin will be there,' Faith continued minutes later. 'I have said you need time to think, and I truly believe that. But *too much* time will be worse. If your feelings are still as strong when you see him at the wedding, don't wait,

Henri. Go ahead and damn well seduce him.' It was Henrietta's turn to stare at her mother in open-mouthed surprise. 'And, whatever you do, *don't* let him convince himself that he's not good for you...'

'Ah cannae deny ah'll be glad tae get back tae Caerlaverock,' Dougal mused. 'But ah reckon the weddin' be a braw way tae finish ma trip off.' They were sitting in the vicarage parlour enjoying a rather nice bottle of best French brandy – a parting gift from the Montclair cellars. Or rather, Dougal was enjoying it – the Reverend had managed barely more than a glass.

'You don't have to wait until the deuced wedding,' the clergyman muttered as he watched the Scot help himself to yet another tipple.

'Ah wouldnae miss it fer the world,' Dougal grinned, sitting back down with a sigh. 'Ah be grateful tae ye, Augustus, fer showin' me true that some Sassenachs be more than lyin', thievin', heathens.'

'Think nothing of it,' the Reverend commented sourly. He looked up at a sudden crash coming from upstairs, wondering what Agnes had smashed now.

She hadn't spoken to him since discovering he'd gone to France without her, and Dougal's comment about her mere presence setting back Anglo-French relationships thirty years certainly hadn't helped the matter. So now she wasn't speaking to either of them.

Which simply proved to the Reverend that the Almighty always provided a silver lining along with every problem – since he'd only have to speak to Dougal between now and the wedding.

He just hoped Agnes wouldn't break his entire collection of snuffboxes in the meantime.

Twenty-Two

'Ah cannae believe the King himself be here,' Finn breathed in awe as he watched his majesty take his place near the front of the church. 'Who be that cove wi' him?'

'I think that's the King's Gentleman Usher - Lord Castleford,' Percy answered.

'What be one o' them?' the boy asked, peering at the ramrod back sitting close to the King.

'He serves in the Royal household,' Lizzy explained and 'looks after the King.'

'But he be a *Lord*,' Finn retorted, giving his mother a puzzled look. 'Ah niver kenned a Lord tae be lookin efter the King, even if he *be* the King.'

'It's a very privileged position,' his father explained. 'Lord Castleton is a very fortunate man.'

'Ah dinnae think he be fortunate tae be wiping the King's arse,' Finn scoffed.

'Finn!' Lizzy admonished the boy in a heated whisper. 'That's quite enough. No more speaking.'

Raphael wasn't sure whether it was the presence of the King that had resulted in Northwood's church being filled to bursting, or the fact that word of the young Marquis de Montclair's return had got out much more rapidly than they'd imagined. Either way, the number of guests far outstripped the church's capacity, and a goodly number of them certainly hadn't been invited – including his majesty.

Rafe gritted his teeth. The whole affair was rapidly becoming an operational nightmare, prompting the Viscount to growl that even if the Queen of bloody Sheba arrived wanting to attend the wedding breakfast, she was to be turned away. It was family only – except for the King, of course.

The King's agent looked round the beautiful old church. Originally built in Norman times, it had been in almost continual use by the Atwood family, and despite the crush, it still held a hushed peace in its very stones. Reverend Shackleford was already up in the pulpit, getting ready to conduct his granddaughter's wedding, and Rafe's chest tightened as he inevitably wondered whether the old priest would officiate at Henrietta's too.

Would it be with him?

There was no doubt that over the last three weeks, Raphael had missed Henri more than he could possibly have imagined. He dreamed of her constantly, waking aching and hard night after night. Was this how a green boy felt in the throes of his first love?

He gave a humourless chuckle. In truth, Rafe suspected the only thing he was really inexperienced at was living a bloody *normal* life. But the shadows were as comfortable as they were dangerous…

He looked around again, but still couldn't see Henrietta and suspected she would be attending the bride along with her other cousins. Seconds later, the organ sounded.

The ceremony had been beautiful, and at the end of it, there hadn't been a dry eye in the house, but as soon as the bride and groom left, mayhem took over as a large number of the guests immediately attempted to get closer to the King.

Which actually turned out to be a good thing, since the people involved in the melee were mostly those who hadn't been officially invited. At the end of the day, it proved a simple matter to surround the King and his companion with guards and as soon as the official guests were inside Northwood Court, escort his majesty and Lord Castleton to the wedding breakfast.

After which, they locked the door.

~

Finn couldn't deny he was having an excellent time, though in truth he and Flossy were full to bursting, and there were still three courses to go. The only problem was that after three solid hours, he was getting perilously close to peeing his breeches - he now knew exactly how the Reverend had felt when they were in the tunnels. But given that he was generally accustomed to answering the call of nature next to the nearest bush, the whole being unable to leave the table was more than a bit of a shock. Bouncing up and down on his chair, Finn was becoming frantic.

In desperation, he tapped his mother's arm to get her attention. Lizzy took one look at his red face and gave him permission to leave. Finn needed no additional urging, and seconds later he'd crawled under the table and was sprinting towards the nearest exit, Flossy at his heels...

~

Though they hadn't spoken, Henrietta was acutely aware of Raphael at the other end of the table, and remembering her mother's advice, she'd spent almost the entire meal devising different ways of actually getting the deuced mutton head on his own. Four courses in, she was beginning to despair, and was just wondering whether she should actually consider standing up and making an announcement, when one of the footmen stood at her shoulder and bent his head towards her, declaring discreetly that she was wanted in the library. Frowning, Henri put down her napkin and, after excusing herself to her dinner companions, quickly made her way out of the room.

Minutes later, the same message was given to Raphael...

To Henri's surprise, the library was empty. After hesitating on the threshold, she went over to the fire. It was a cold, blustery day, and the room was undeniably chilly. After a few minutes, she frowned. Any longer, and her absence would be noticed. Who on earth could have wanted to speak with her so urgently? Disquiet set in as she continued to warm her hands.

Seconds later, she heard the door open and swung round... only to see Raphael standing by the door.

They stood regarding each other in silence for a moment, then Henrietta clenched her hands and gritted her teeth. It was now or never.

Determinedly, she stalked towards him, completely unaware of the formidable expression on her face until she got close enough to recognise the apprehension in Raphael's eyes.

She stopped less than a foot away. Still, he said nothing, but his expression had turned resigned. Clearly, the deuced widgeon was expecting a set-down. Henri let her face relax as she took the last step. Did he truly want her? There was only one way to find out...

A mere second later, Henrietta literally threw herself into Raphael's arms. She barely noticed as he fell back after catching her full weight because her mouth was over his, and she was kissing him as though her life depended on it.

With a low groan, Rafe wrapped her into his arms and returned the kiss, turning it into an all-consuming melding of mouths that demanded the complete and utter surrender of both of them.

Driven almost mindless by her soft whimper, he lifted her off her feet, holding her underneath her bottom, pressing her against that part of him that had ached, night after night until he'd finally, helplessly, spilled his seed into his hand. Unconsciously, she lifted her legs, wrapping them around his hips, riding his hardness in an instinct as old as time.

So great was his need that Raphael was quickly losing any sense of right or wrong. Without releasing her lips, his hand slipped between them, pulling at the ribbon tying the edge of her dress. Seconds later her breast was freed to his greedy, searching fingers, and she gasped out loud as he rolled her already enflamed nipple against his thumb before cupping the entire globe in his hand...

'Err... thunder an' turf, don't you think there's a time and place for this sort of thing?'

The Reverend's strident tones halted their passion like a bucket of cold water.

With a muttered expletive, Rafe allowed Henri to slide back to the floor while shielding her with his body as she struggled to adjust her clothing.

'I have no intention of playing the voyeur, or the blabbermouth,' Reverend Shackleford continued sternly, 'but I do expect to see the pair of you back in the dining room before the cheese course.'

Without waiting for their answer, he gave a final hmph, and went back through the door, closing it gently behind him. Once on the other side, he suppressed a grin and gave Dougal the thumbs up. All in all, a very successful half an hour's work...

~

There was no denying that Finn felt like a new person after a few moments spent in the Viscountess's prize rose garden. Indeed, it was almost as if his diminished bladder actually increased his stomach capacity.

Picking Flossy up, the boy happily made his way back to the dining room. As he entered, his first thought was to wonder whether the King was enjoying the scran as much as he was, and his second was whether to go straight for the cheeses or indulge in the syllabub first.

And his third thought... What the devil was Lord Castleton doing furtively pouring the contents of a small vial into the goblet in front of him?

Finn approached the Gentleman Usher slowly, watching with interest. A few seconds later, his lordship glanced around before picking up a spoon and using it to nonchalantly stir the contents of the goblet.

Frowning, the boy drew closer, just as the Lord Castleton tapped his spoon on the side of the goblet. The sleeve of his jacket fell back, revealing a large scar beginning at his thumb.

Finn froze. With a thrill of sudden terror, he realised he'd never thought to mention the scar he'd seen on *Mr Top Hat man's* hand... The scar that was exactly the same as the one on Lord Castleton's hand.

But Lord Pemberton was *Mr Top Hat man* – everyone said so.

Finn's heart was racing as he watched Lord Castleton hand the goblet to the King. Watched his majesty raise it to his lips...

'*Stop*,' he screamed out loud, a sense of unreality exploding around him. Everyone turned - everyone but Lord Castleton, who was busy urging King William to finish his drink.

'Dinnae drink that, yer majesty,' he yelled, starting to run, 'lest ye want tae be deid wi' poisinin'.'

Lord Castleton pushed his chair back, spluttering, 'What in devil's name is the stupid boy shouting about? Is he addled?'

'Dinnae touch it, yer majesty,' Finn repeated desperately as he finally reached the King. 'It be poisoned. By him.' He pointed towards the Gentleman Usher, who reacted by jumping to his feet and grabbing the boy by his jacket.

'Unhand him.' The order came from Percy, who jumped to his feet, his face as livid as anyone had ever seen it.

'The boy should be locked up,' Castleton sneered, thrusting Finn away in contempt. 'I'm not staying here listening to addlebrained accusations.' He turned to storm out.

'You drink it.' The words were not spoken loudly but were nevertheless heard by everyone. King William held out the goblet and repeated his request.

For a few frozen moments, Lord Castleton looked at the goblet, then, without warning, he kicked his chair out of the way and sprinted towards the door.

The same door that Raphael and Henrietta were just entering. As the fleeing Usher charged towards him, Raphael acted instinctively. Pushing Henri behind him, he stood with his feet wide apart and seconds later planted the oncoming noble a prime facer that would be talked about for years.

Fortunately, since nearly all the guests were of the Shackleford variety, nobody swooned and certainly nobody wanted to miss dessert.

Twenty-Three

An hour later, his knuckles wrapped in a cloth, Raphael waited for an audience with the King. He wasn't alone. Also seated in the room were Nicholas, Roan, Tristan, Gabriel, and Henrietta. As the only woman, Henri had no idea why she'd been summoned, but she was content to simply remain near Raphael after making a vow to herself not to let the imbecile out of her sight ever again...

Two hours later, the King finally emerged, having apparently had forty winks followed by a nice long soak in the bath. Only narrowly escaping being poisoned by one's closest confidante had undoubtedly left his majesty a little shaken...

After seating himself comfortably, King William turned to his lead agent. 'Perhaps you can enlighten me as to why you arrested one lord, while allowing another to very nearly kill your sovereign?'

Raphael winced. 'We had believed Lord Pemberton to be the leader of the conspiracy. There was no reason to suspect another – especially one so close to you, Your Majesty.'

Raphael was well aware that his explanation was no excuse, but in truth he didn't have one. If it hadn't been for Finn, the King might even now be dead.

'As I understand it, Augustin. You simply fudged it, did you not?' After a moment, Rafe sighed and nodded.

King William crossed his legs, regarding his chief agent balefully. 'You have always thought yourself invulnerable, Raphael. Incapable of making a mistake, but after today, I have to conclude you have lost your touch.'

Rafe didn't know how to answer - he didn't *have* an answer. How could he argue when, minutes before the King was in peril, he was making love with the woman who had taken over his very world?

Henrietta opened her mouth to speak, but her father took hold of her arm, warning her that now was not the time for heroics.

The King got to his feet. 'I am hereby releasing you from your duties,' he declared formally. 'From this moment on, you are no longer the head of my intelligence.'

'You're casting me out?' Rafe couldn't have stopped the accusation if hell had taken him.

King William raised his eyebrows, then he shook his head and sighed.

'For God's sake, Raphael, marry your young lady. Go and have lots of babies. Live a life free of secrets. And while you're at it, get rid of that bloody poker you've had up your arse for the last however many years...' He turned and headed towards the door, before suddenly stopping. Seconds later he turned and strode back to his former agent, laying a hand on his shoulder.

'You've been first my brother's eyes and ears, and then mine for most of your adult life. That will not change. The only difference is that you will no longer be my sword.

'Go and live your life, Rafe. I believe Lord Castleton has a rather splendid house in the hills above Torquay. Clearly, he's not going to have much use for it, so it's yours - payment for services rendered. I'll have the papers drawn up tomorrow.'

Seconds later he was gone, leaving the whole room in silence.

'Are you willing to marry a man without an income?' Raphael murmured hoarsely to Henrietta a few moments later. In answer, she threw herself into his arms for the second time in as many hours.

On the other side of the room, her father gave a low chuckle. 'In fairness, now that Tris has taken a step up in the world, I am actually looking for a new business partner...'

THE END

Francesca - Book 5 of The Shackleford Legacies will be released in late 2026.

If you'd like me to let you know as soon as it's available, and receive a FREE short story introducing The Shackleford Sisters, copy and paste the link below into your browser to sign up to my newsletter and I'll keep you updated about *Francesca* and all my latest releases.

https://motivated-teacher-3299.kit.com/143a008c18

Keeping in Touch

Thank you so much for reading *Henrietta,* I really hope you enjoyed it. For any of you who'd like to connect, I'd really love to hear from you. Feel free to contact me via my facebook page:
https://www.facebook.com/beverleywattsromanticcomedyauthor
or my website:
http://www.beverleywatts.com

As I said earlier, if you'd like me to let you know as soon as *Francesca - Book 5 of The Shackleford Legacies* is available, and receive a FREE short story introducing The Shackleford Sisters, copy and paste the link below into your browser to sign up to my newsletter and I'll keep you updated about that and all my latest releases.

https://motivated-teacher-3299.kit.com/143a008c18

And lastly, if you're enjoying the Shackleford world and don't want to wait until *Francesca* is released, you might be interested to know that I have recently begun a new series featuring the Victorian Shacklefords. The series is titled *Shackleford and Daughters* and Book One is called *Alexandra*. Keep reading for a sneak peek...

Alexandra

Prologue

'Aunt Charlotte, what on earth do you think you're doing?' Alexandra Shackleford watched in helpless horror as her maiden aunt lifted her skirts and attempted to thrust one stocking-clad leg through the narrow opening in the cellar window.

'How the devil do you think we're going to unmask the charlatan if we don't know what she knows?' the spinster retorted, 'and don't call me Aunt.'

'I really don't think there are any *suitable* gentlemen within hearing distance,' Alex retorted. 'At least I hope not, else they'll be calling the constabulary.'

'I am most assuredly not happy about this,' Henry Shackleford declared heatedly, wincing as his sister snagged her drawers on the sill. 'I am attending the séance in two days' time as we discussed, and I'm entirely convinced our suspect has plenty of reasons to consider me a prime candidate for blackmail.'

'Damn and blast,' Charlotte swore, trying to unhook her frilly bloomers. 'But what about the others? All those muttonheads she already managed to snare? I've said from the beginning - if we don't discover who she's swindling and what hold she has over them, we won't have the rat entirely cornered.'

'May I remind you once again, Charlotte, that *breaking and entering is against the law,*' her brother retorted, finally on the brink of losing his temper. 'I am entirely opposed to this foolhardiness. It's reckless in the extreme.'

'Well, it's about time you indulged in a spot of recklessness,' Charlotte flung back, rattling the catch in frustration, 'It's all very well you prattling endlessly on about the law, but you've been following it to the deuced letter for thirty years and look where it's got you.' She gave her drawers another sharp tug, adding, 'Truly Henry, how you ever got to Chief Inspector is beyond me. You've got the instincts of an aspidistra.' She gave a final, frustrated yank, and her drawers came free with an ominous ripping sound. 'Bugger,' she muttered, pulling her leg back out and nearly falling over in the process.

'I don't think now is quite the time for bickering,' Alexandra interrupted. 'Clearly you are not going to get through that window Charlotte, and if you make any more noise, you're likely to wake the entire household.'

'I'm almost certain the house is empty,' her aunt retorted. 'You watched our so-called medium climb onto the London train not twelve hours ago. I expect she'll be returning early tomorrow.'

'That doesn't mean that awful old woman's not in the house,' Alex countered.

'You said you thought her as deaf as a post. So stop dithering, Alexandra, and climb in through this window. As much as it pains me to say it, you're a little more agile than me.'

'And two stone lighter.' Alex's retort was muttered under her breath as she reluctantly picked up her skirts and stepped carefully to the small window opening into the cellar. Once there, she peered in through the grimy glass.

'Charlotte, this has gone on quite long enough,' Henry snapped. 'It's quite one thing for you to be locked up, but I am most certainly *not* having my eldest daughter being charged with a criminal offence.' Both women turned around in astonishment.

'Why is it of no consequence if I am locked up?' Charlotte protested indignantly.

Henry didn't answer. Instead, he placed his valise determinedly on the ground. 'If there is any offence to be committed, I will do it,' he announced, unbuttoning his jacket and carefully removing it. After folding and placing it on top of the valise, he rolled up his sleeves and glared at his sister.

'Right then, Lottie, you'll need to give me a leg up.'

Chapter One

Paignton, England, two months earlier...

At nearly two and twenty, Alexandra Shackleford was no longer a child. Unfortunately, her father was not quite of the same opinion. Consequently, she was forced into the ignominious position of listening outside the study door in order to discover exactly why he'd been given notice from the Exeter Police Force after thirty years of exemplary service. At least that was what she'd always been told. In those exact words. *Exemplary Service.*

Unfortunately, one of the side-effects of adulthood was discovering that truths one had always believed inviolate, turned out on occasion to be entirely fabricated.

Indeed, her Aunt Charlotte's colourful description of her father's policing career could certainly never be repeated in polite company.

'What in thunderation are you doing, Alex?' Her twin sister Arabella's notion of adulthood was more of the, *I'm now old enough to wear silk stockings*, ilk. Listening at doors held no interest for her unless it was to discover whether her father was in favour of her attending the Oldway Mansion Summer Ball. Especially as it was rumoured that Mr Washington Singer would be present this year with his new wife.

'Did you know Papa was dismissed from his job?' Alex hissed, grabbing her sister's arm and pulling her away from the door.

'What poppycock,' Bella scoffed. 'He retired. They even gave him that hideous carriage clock on the parlour mantelpiece.'

Alexandra shook her head. 'He's in the study with Aunt Charlotte now. Apparently, the Chief Commissioner's son was accused of...' She paused and frowned, before continuing, 'I couldn't quite hear what, but anyway, Papa insisted on questioning him at the station and Sir Drayton got to hear of it, and...'

'They had an almighty collie shangle,' Arabella finished.

Alex nodded. 'Apparently everyone in the station heard the argument. In the end, Papa was given the choice of retiring or being dismissed.'

'Well, they gave him the carriage clock, so that must mean he wasn't *actually* dismissed,' Arabella countered. 'Clearly, he chose to retire.' She gave a shrug. 'Papa is even older than Aunt Charlotte, so perhaps it will be good for him.'

'But what on earth is he going to do? He'll be at home with the seven women, and that's not counting Mrs Williams or Peggy.'

'He'll doubtless lock himself in here,' Arabella stated pragmatically, nodding towards the closed door. Then she grinned. 'Mrs Williams will leave his meals outside until eventually, when they stop disappearing, Aunt Charlotte will force open the door and find him, stiff as a board at his desk.'

'Don't be so macabre, and anyway, what about Agatha? I doubt very much she'll be content to be a permanent fixture in the study.'

'No, you're right. Then perhaps Papa will take her for long walks on

Roundham Head. He'll be like Heathcliff, wandering the cliffs, bemoaning the loss of his one true love.'

Alex snorted. 'I assume you mean Papa, not Aggie – and I'm not sure Heathcliff had a dog. Anyway, Mama may have been his one true love, but she died over ten years ago now. If he unexpectedly starts wandering, it will be because he's suddenly taken leave of his senses.'

'If you ask Aunt Charlotte, there's nothing sudden about it. She'll tell you he did that years ago.'

The two girls giggled just as the door was thrown open to reveal the aunt in question. She eyed them both narrowly, before stepping into the hall and pulling the door shut behind her. 'I take it you've been listening for long enough to know that your father has been forcibly retired from the police force.'

Both girls blinked, not quite sure how to answer. At length, Alex gave a small cough and murmured, 'Well, at least he'll no longer be at the whim of Sir Drayton.'

Their Aunt humphed and ushered them away from the closed door. 'That may well be, and I cannot deny that being finally unchained from that festering pustule can be anything other than a good thing. But retire? What the devil is the chucklehead going to do with himself stuck in a house with seven deuced women day after day?' The matron threw her hands in the air after unknowingly repeating her niece's just-voiced concerns.

'Well, Billy comes in daily, and then there's Albert.'

'Billy is nine years old,' Charlotte declared. 'And Albert couldn't string a coherent sentence together if his life depended on it. Though your father's level of conversation might be considered less than sparkling, I believe even he needs a little more stimulation than that.'

'What about the Paignton Club?'

Charlotte pursed her lips. 'Fifty members, and they haven't got an original thought between them.'

Alex and Bella looked at each other. They both knew their Aunt's dislike of the Paignton Club was simply because it only allowed supposed *gentlemen* past its hallowed doors. Since that had been the way of the world for as long as they could remember, neither twin could understand Charlotte's aversion to this particular Gentleman's club. Alex vowed that one day she'd pluck up the courage to ask her.

Charlotte Shackleford had arrived at the front door of Cliff House less than a month after their mother had inadvertently fallen to her death whilst looking for a rare Cormorant's nest.

Alexandra and Arabella had been eleven years old at the time. The eldest of three sets of twins. The second set, Beatrix and Bernice, had been eight, and Florence and Daisy barely seven. Samuel and Nicholas, the two boys in the family, were less affected. At seventeen, Samuel had already joined the Royal Navy, and Nicholas, at fifteen, had already begun an apprenticeship at a local solicitor's office.

The girls had never met anybody like her before. Aunt Charlotte was ill-tempered, uncompromising and exceedingly outspoken. Within forty-eight hours of her appearance, her recently widowed brother Henry had declared unequivocally that it wasn't any wonder she'd remained unwed, since any man would have to be a complete and utter clodpole to leg shackle himself to such a termagant.

Such insults were like water off a duck's back to Charlotte, who declared herself completely indifferent to the prospect of matrimony. Nevertheless, despite her nonchalance, it had to be said that her mere presence continued to strike terror within the heart of every male in the seaside town of Paignton with a pulse – especially if he happened to be single. Her tendency to swear like the navvies responsible for building the recent railway as well as her distressing proclivity for calling a spade a spade were the two final nails in her marital coffin.

So, Charlotte stayed, along with the carriage she arrived in, Albert the coachman and two lazy horses named Max and Ned. All in all, it was safe to say that life for the Shacklefords of Cliff House was never the same again.

Alexandra - Book One of Shackleford and Daughters is available from Amazon

Turn the page for a complete list of my books on Amazon...

Also available by Beverley Watts on Amazon

The Shackleford Sisters (1806-1828)

Book 1 - Grace

Book 2 - Temperance

Book 3 - Faith

Book 4 - Hope

Book 5 - Patience

Book 6 - Charity

Book 7 - Chastity

Book 8 - Prudence

Book 9 - Anthony

The Shackleford Legacies (1830 onwards)

Book 1 - Jennifer

Book 2 - Mercedes

Book 3 - Roseanna

Book 4 - Henrietta

Book 5 - Francesca coming in 2026

Shackleford and Daughters (1891 onwards)

Book 1 - Alexandra

Book 2 - Arabella will be released on 30th April 2026

The Shackleford Diaries (Present Day)

Book 1 - Claiming Victory
Book 2 - Sweet Victory
Book 3 - All For Victory
Book 4 - Chasing Victory
Book 5 - Lasting Victory
Book 6 - A Shackleford Victory
Book 7 - Final Victory

The Admiral Shackleford Mysteries (Present Day)

Book 1 - A Murderous Valentine
Book 2 - A Murderous Marriage
Book 3 - A Murderous Season

Standalone Titles (Present Day)

An Officer and a Gentleman Wanted

About the Author

Beverley Watts

Beverley spent 8 years teaching English as a Foreign Language to International Military Students in Britannia Royal Naval College, the Royal Navy's premier officer training establishment in the UK. She says that in the whole 8 years there was never a dull moment and many of her wonderful experiences at the College were not only memorable but were most definitely 'the stuff of fiction.' Her debut novel An Officer And A

Gentleman Wanted is very loosely based on her adventures at the College.

Beverley particularly enjoys writing books that make people laugh and currently she has four series of Romantic Comedies, both contemporary and historical, as well as a humorous cosy mystery series under her belt.

She lives with her husband in an apartment overlooking the sea on the beautiful English Riviera. Between them they have 3 adult children and two gorgeous grandchildren plus a menagerie of animals including 4 Romanian rescue dogs of indeterminate breed called Florence, Trixie, Lizzie and Aggie.
Until recently they also had an adorable 'Chichon' named Dotty who was the inspiration for Dotty in The Shackleford Diaries.

You can find out more about Beverley's books at
http://www.beverleywatts.com

Printed in Dunstable, United Kingdom

76434067R00118